A Garland Series

The
Flowering of the Novel

Representative Mid-Eighteenth Century Fiction
1740-1775

A Collection of 121 Titles

Memoirs of
a Man of Honour

Abbé Prévost

Garland Publishing, Inc., New York & London

1975

Bibliographical note:

this facsimile has been made from a copy in the
Bodleian Library of Oxford University
(249.s.781)

Library of Congress Cataloging in Publication Data

Prévost, Antoine François, called Prévost d'Exiles,
    1697-1763.
    Memoirs of a man of honour.

    (The Flowering of the novel)
    Translation of Memoires d'un honnête homme.
    Reprint of the 1747 ed. printed for J. Nourse, London.
    I. Title.   II. Series.
PZ3.P929Me15   [PQ2021.M4]   843'.5   74-23659
ISBN 0-8240-1119-8

Printed in the United States of America

MEMOIRS

OF A

MAN

OF

HONOUR.

Translated from the *French*.

PART I.

L O N O N:

Printed for John Nourse, over-againſt
Katherine-ſtreet in the *Strand.*
MDCCXLVII.

THE

Editor's PREFACE.

IT would be unpardonable to present the public, with a work of this nature, without subjoining some account of the author, and by what means it came into my hands.

About two years since, I went from Brussels to Italy, with an English nobleman, whom I had the honour to accompany in the tour he made: being considered as meer travellers, we had no other trouble than shewing our passports, through great part of Germany, but this facility diminished, as we entered the Tyrolese: at every walled town, we were obliged to be conducted

to

to the governor, and explain the motives which had brought us into the province.

The name of Englishmen, however, attracted many civilities: we had more than once the advantage of being invited to houses where we past the night more agreeably than in the wretched inns of Germany.

The governor of Infpruc, was the third, from whom we received this obligation: he is the fon of Baron Traftef, who refided at London, for feveral years, in quality of minifter of Vienna. He preffed us fo much to ftay fome days with him, that we could not in gratitude and good manners refufe him.

We could not fpeak the German language, but he underftood Italian, which was familiar to us. Thus being obliged to converfe in a foreign tongue, he could not diftinguifh that I was French.

Among many other amufements, he procured for us, he fhewed us the caftle of Infpruc, which is well fortified, and capable

*capable of making a good defence. Be-
ing conducted by him into a garden
formed into terrasses, on the ramparts,
we perceived a man of a very graceful
appearance walking alone, unarmed, and
followed by a soldier, with his sword by
his side, and his fuzee upon his shoulder.
The governor prevented the questions our
curiosity might have made; that, said
he, is a* French *prisoner, who, six
months ago, when I took possession of my post,
I found confined in the Dungeon, in a
most miserable condition. They told me
he had been stopped for want of a pass-
port, within some leagues of* Inspruc,
*and his answers, when examin'd, be-
ing unsatisfactory, he was brought hither as a spy.*

The Court of Vienna *has been informed in what manner he was seized,
but not having leisure to think on so
trifling an affair, had sent no orders
concerning him, to my predecessor.*

I do not understand French, *continued the governor, but by the account
some persons who know that language*

give

give of him, as well as by his phisiognomy, I am perswaded, that he is a
man of distinction.

I have allowed him what liberty you
see, while I wait the pleasure of the
court, and have not refused him paper
and books. He has also desired permission to write to M. the M. de B. who is
at Frankfort, but I know not yet whether
it would be proper to grant it.

This discourse made an impression on
the young English nobleman, almost e-
qual to my own; and as we had agreed,
that I should not be known for a French-
man, he told the governor, that as we
could speak a little of that language,
we should be glad to talk a moment or
two with the prisoner, if he found it
not inconvenient to grant us that liberty.

To which he readily consented. I was
the first that accosted this illustrious unfortunate, who was extremely surprised
to find himself saluted by one of his own
nation; but I told him in a few words,
the

the precautions we had to take, and of-
fered him all the service in my power.

He maintained no reserve, after know-
ing I was French, *and sensible of the*
advantage this opportunity might afford
him, discovered to me his name, and the
melancholy reasons which had drawn on
him this misfortune, after having made
him quit his country. He mentioned
several ways by which he might be re-
lieved, if it were not better, added he,
to suffer a wretch to perish, whose life
is become odious to him.

His name was not unknown to me. I
endeavoured to console him with the
hopes of better fortune, and seeing the English *lord seemed touched with his situa-*
tion, I entreated that young nobleman
to recommend him to baron Trastef.

We desired the favour of seeing his
prison, and found it a decent chamber,
the window of which afforded only the
prospect of a frightful chain of moun-
tains; but after having described the
horrors of that dungeon he had ex-
changed

changed for it, he affured me, that he
thought himfelf much indebted to the
goodnefs and generofity of the new governor.

He had feveral books, both French
and Latin; but feeing fome papers, which
appeared to be manufcripts, I had the
curiofity to afk what was the fubject of
his meditations.

He confeffed, that being full of the
accidents which had ruin'd his fortune,
and his repofe, he had found a little
eafe for fome months paft, in writing
them, as they occurred to his remembrance.

There were two manufcripts, one of
which I perceived, was but a fair copy of the other. The lively intereft I
took in his affairs, made me, perhaps,
a little indifcreet.

I entreated him, if reafons too powerful did not oppofe my requeft, to be-
ftow on me one of thofe copies, engaging at
the fame time, my faith, and my honour,

to

to do nothing with it, but for his own advantage.

Tho' I was not of a family could be known to him, I told him the post I held, about a young man of the most high birth, might give him some idea of my character. I then mentioned some of my friends, who, on divers circumstances, had obtained the esteem of many worthy persons, who were capable of serving him.

He shewed much less difficulty than I expected in agreeing to my proposal. My air, and my discourse, he said, bespoke me a man of integrity, and he would depend on the prejudice he had in my favour. Besides, how could I undertake any thing for his service, if I did not know the means of doing it by the history of his life?

He annexed only three conditions to the grant of my request, which were, not to permit his manuscript to be printed, without the consent of a lady, who was the principal character in it. To
retrench

retrench all she was not willing should be published, and to suppress the names of some known persons.

I submitted with the most solemn oath, to three such reasonable injunctions, and there remained nothing now but to deceive the governor's eyes, in order to avoid useless explanations, which I did, by putting the manuscript in my pocket, just as he turned to go out of the room.

What services they were which my gratitude and esteem presently made me undertake, does not belong to this Preface.

I continued my travels, and am still in Italy; *but after having, in that distance, found means which is not yet a fit time to explain, but which have happily succeeded to my hopes, I hear that the lady, on whom the publication of the work depended, has been dead some months, on which I think myself discharged of the two first conditions, the other concerning the names I have fulfilled.*

The

The manuscript is gone to Paris, *where I leave it to the press; it will nevertheless be revised by* M. le Chev. de V * *, *whose interest in the family, will make him careful in the examination, and who is capable of embellishing the stile with those graces, which is it less furnished with, than just sentiments and manners. All I reserve to myself, is the title, in which I wish no alteration may be made. It is my own; and as I am under an obligation not to name the author, I know nothing so agreeable to the impression his person and his principles have made on me, as the title* Of a Man of Honour.

Memoirs

BOOKS Printed for J. NOURSE, at the Lamb against Katherine-street, in the Strand.

I. THE *Royal English* Grammar, containing what is necessary to the Knowledge of the *English* Tongue, laid down in a plain and familiar Way. For the use of young Gentlemen and Ladies. *To which are added,* Lessons for Boys at School, shewing the use of the Parts of Speech, and the joining Words together in a Sentence. By *JAMES GREEN-WOOD, Sur-Master of St Paul's School.* The Second Edition. *Beautifully printed in a neat pocket Volume.* Price bound 1s. 6d. *Recommended by Dr.* S. Clark, *Dr.* Waterland, *and Dr.* J. Watts. *Dedicated to, and designed for the use of her Royal Highness the Princess of* Wales.

II. Instructive and Entertaining NOVELS; designed to promote *Vertue, good Sense,* and *universal Benevolence.* Enrich'd with great variety of curious and uncommon *Incidents* and *Events,* exceeding *pleasant* and *profitable.* Translated from the *Original Spanish* of the inimitable *M. Cervantes,* Author of *Don Quixot.* By *Thomas Shelton.* With an account of the *Work,* by a *Gentleman* of the *Middle-Temple.*

III. A Tour through the *Animal World;* or an historical and accurate Account of near 400 Animals, Birds, Fishes, Serpents, Insects, &*c.* describing their different Natures, Qualities and Use, as well for the common Service and Food of Man, as his Diversions and Cure of his Maladies. Extracted from *Gesner, Willoughby, Swammerdam, Mouffet, Meriam,* and others the most celebrated Authors upon this Subject. To which is added a Description of some of the most rare and curious Productions of the Vegetable World. *The whole enrich'd with an entire new Set of Copper Plates, representing each Quadrupede, Bird, Fish, Insect, and Plant. By the Chevalier* Denis de Coetlogon, *M. D. Knight of the Order of St. Lazare, and Member of the Royal Academy of Angers.* 12mo. Price bound 3s. 6d.

MEMOIRS

OF A

MAN *of* HONOUR.

I Come from a deep and horrid dungeon, where I have paſſed three weeks without ſeeing light; faſtened to the wall by a huge chain, which, encompaſſing my body, ſcarce allowed me to ſit down. Thoſe from whom I received this cruel treatment, have ſuppoſed me guilty of crimes of which I am ignorant: I have only ſuffered for want of being better known; for my heart has nothing wherewith to reproach itſelf: —— Innocence and ill-fortune have been the inſeparable companions of my whole life.

B   Mʏ

My fituation is now more tollerable:
—— they have removed me to a chamber in the caftle of *Infpruck*, and relea-
fed me from my fetters; but I am as
little acquainted with the motive of their
prefent pity, as of their late feverity.
—— I am ignorant even of the language
they fpeak here: the foldiers, or rather
boors, appointed to guard me, appear
to be *Germans*; but comprehending by
their figns, that I am allowed the liberty
of the garden, I walk fome turns in it
every day, yet cannot fay, I find any o-
ther benefit from this condefcention,
than that of exercife; there being little
elegance in the parterres, or terraffes,
with which it is compofed, and the profpect very confined. Seldom, therefore,
I wait for a fignal from the foldier, that
attends me, to retire; and find more a-
mufement in my chamber, when looking through the iron grates of my win-
dows, I furvey thofe huge barren moun-
tains, with which the city of *Infpruck*
is environed. Here I behold a great
number of fhepherds, who, while their
flocks are feeding, either fit or loll on the
fides of the hills, never rifing, unlefs to
gather

gather flowers, or play upon their ruſtic inſtruments. —— How can theſe people be called unhappy, whoſe indolence and ſupineneſs ſhews them entirely free from all anxiety and care!

How different the condition of my mind! a thouſand ſad remembrances had doubtleſs thrown me into the moſt dreadful deſpair, if heaven had not inſpired me with the thought of entreating ſome books with which I might beguile diſtreſs, and paſs ſome of thoſe long and languiſhing hours that hung ſo heavily on me. The ſigns I made for this purpoſe were underſtood, and the next day ſeveral *Latin* and *French* treatiſes were brought to me, with a proviſion of ink and paper, which I received as the moſt precious treaſure. My confinement now became more ſupportable; I am abandon'd of mankind, ſaid I, and have loſt even the hope of ever being otherwiſe, ſince denied permiſſion to write to thoſe who might intereſt themſelves in my liberty : but this reflection ought to moderate my deſires, and reaſon enable me to make a virtue of neceſſity: if I am condemned to paſs the remainder of my

days

days in the castle of *Inspruck*, what will
it avail me to preserve the memory of
things past, or to form new ideas of the
future? All my measures are broke! all
my views are at an end! I must regard
myself as already separated from a world,
where I no longer have any thing to
pretend. In fine, I am the same as dead,
when all the ways for returning to the
conversation of the living are shut against
me.

My spirits, thus benumbed, as it were,
with the melancholly that oppressed me,
I was very near sinking into that lethargic stupidity I had observed in the poor
shepherds, when I begun to turn over
my books; but I soon perceived this was
not a disposition in which I could hope
to·reap any advantage by reading; and
my reason now contradicting what it
had before suggested, reminded me, that
the only way not to live, was not to meditate. On this, the few remains I had of
fortitude collected themselves, and joined
to rouze my late inactive faculties; and,
as what was most interesting to myself,
was most likely to preserve my attention,
I resolved to recall the images of my past
adventures;

adventures; and, in doing so, began by degrees to judge in a different manner of those accidents, from the memory of which I had lately wished to be delivered. The effort I made, succeeded; and I am now convinced, that there is nothing fortifies a man against despair, so much as the contemplation of those objects which have heretofore engrossed him. This is a satisfaction which a prison cannot shut out. This I have determined to enjoy; and if, in recollecting the circumstances of my past life, some unpleasing incidents may arise, even the pain they give brings comfort with it, since the very worst of evils is to be insensible.

Thus shall I employ the paper has been allowed me, and for this purpose I take up the pen. ——— It will give little trouble to my memory to bring back those accidents, which, like a chain, have been all linked together by their cause, and proceed from the same source: a love, perhaps, beyond measure of truth and justice, unhappily joined with the weakness of a heart too tender, has occasioned all the calamities of

my

my life : my whole character is comprehended in thefe words, and the proofs of many years has fufficiently fhewn me, I have no neceffity of examining farther into myfelf.

These emotions were from my very infancy difcernable : a man of great underftanding in human nature, who had the care of my education, obferving that I gave myfelf up to pleafure with the utmoft eagernefs and vivacity, yet, neverthelefs, nothing was more eafy than to recover me into the moft ferious reflections, ufed frequently to fay, that between two inclinations fo different, which ever got the better, would certainly be carried to a very great excefs; and if any equality was preferved, I muft be born to be the moft unfortunate of all men; which laft prediction has been but too fadly verified.

I came into the world with all the advantages of birth and fortune : the death of an uncle, who left me all his effects, rendered me independant on my family at twenty years of age. My father, after having honourably acquitted himfelf in one

one of the first posts in the army, had retired to his country seat, and was rejoyced
to see me in a condition to live in a handsome manner, without any assistance from
his revenue. He seldom interfered with
any schemes I formed for my advance-
ment, farther than to wish me success,
and give me his advice; but I often observed, that he testified somewhat of an
unusual earnestness in that he gave me of
going to settle for some time at *Paris.*
He being a widower, and desirous of
marrying again, had been with-held meerly by the considerations of my interest,
which consideration ceasing on my uncle's
estate devolving on me, he thought himself at liberty to pursue his inclinations,
and waited only for my departure, to es-
pouse with more decency, a young lady
of about three or four and twenty years
of age. I was so far nevertheless from
foreseeing this marriage, that some little
time before I left the country, I had felt
some slight tokens of a Passion, for the
very person who was intended for my
mother-in-law; and found the particular
respect I treated her with was not in the
least disagreeable; but all this was no more
than the transient ideas of youth and ga-

iety,

iety, which the thoughts of my journey immediately after diffipated, and when I arrived at *Paris*, I heard the refolution my father had made, with lefs trouble, than aftonifhment.

THE city of *Paris* was not altogether new to me, I had paft feveral years there, but then it was either in the college or a-cademy, under the direction of a wife go-vernor, who knew how to reftrain me to the limits befitting my age.----I was not however, at my fecond coming, much at a lofs how to conduct myfelf, being about fixteen when I returned to my father; the converfation of the moft polite men of that province had fafhioned my behaviour and manners, fo as to render me capable of appearing with an air of freedom a-mong the beft of company. He was a man of honour and merit, and having been forty years in the fervice, where many gallant actions had raifed him to the degree of a *field-marfhal* : he was treated by the whole country with an efteem and veneration, of which myfelf, as his fon, felt the effects.   His levee was every day crowded with a number of brave officers, who like him had retired after their long
fervices,

fervices, and who all refpected him as their chief: fo that between them, many gentlemen in the neighbourhood, who had lefs of the goods of fortune with the fame birth; prelates and other ecclefiaftics our houfe was continually full. That noble eafe and freedom with which my father accompanied his entertainments, made it indeed a kind of little court, where wit and chearfulnefs gave a double relifh to the elegance of the table. In taking leave of this fcene of tranquility, I had letters of recommendation to feveral friends, whofe names were all at that time I knew of them; but the moft material among them, were thofe to the general officers who had ferved with my father; it being my inclination and intent to apply myfelf entirely to the ftudy of military affairs; though fomething the *Intendant* of our provence had wrote to his family concerning me, occafioned my falling into company which engaged me too far in purfuits of a different nature.

THE next day after my arrival I was obliged to accept of an entertainment, at the houfe of our *Intendant*'s lady, where the guefts were very numerous: they

B 5   treated

treated me as a perſon who was unacquainted with the modes of *Paris*, and every one thought it would be an obligation to me to be better informed. I preſently found a deſign was formed to attach me to this ſociety, by all ſorts of gallantries and carreſſes, nor did I feel the leaſt repugnance in myſelf to it. The ladies were extremely amiable, and the men had wit and ſpirit, and were moſt of them gentlemen of the long robe, or had offices in the treaſury. I found among them more of warmth and vehemence, than I had obſerved in thoſe of the country; but the attention I was obliged to give, in order to comprehend the meaning of a thouſand things they ſaid, prevented me at firſt from making much reflections on the manner in which they were expreſſed. Here I was told the current hiſtories of the town; the modes; the pleaſures; the character of new books, and theatrical performances; the criticiſms; the panegyrics; the ſatyrs, and the judgment of all ſort of people, were repeated by ſome one or other of this aſſembly. The multiplicity of theſe ſubjects was not unknown to me, but the way in which they were treated, appeared altogether ſtrange to me.

me. The relating openly certain facts which seemed to require the greatest secrecy, and the positive decision I found given in divers points which I thought not well understood, gave me a good deal of surprize; however I imputed it rather to my own ignorance, than their self-sufficiency, and readily yielded my assent to many things which I knew nothing of. Before we separated, many parties of pleasure were proposed, which I accepted of, and that same evening engaged myself to sup at seven different houses successively.

I T was so late when they began to speak of retiring, that I had little desire of any thing but repose. The next morning however, I considered that good manners obliged me to wait on madam the *Intendant*'s lady, not only to pay my respects to her, but also to learn from her something of the characters of those persons with whom I was to sup, and who had shewn so great an earnestness in obliging me. It was towards noon when I went to her house, and she spared me the trouble of asking those things I desired to know, by the impatience she felt

B 6   herself

herself to repeat them to me. Are not
you afraid, *said she laughing*, that we
have a design to engrofs you too much,
by finding your felf engaged all at once
for feven days? but I underftood by my
husbands letter, that you would not be
forry to make fome acquaintance, and I
therefore affembled a part of mine. I do
not tell you, *continued she*, that they are
all of equal merit, for it would be too
great a happinefs to find ten or twelve
perfons fuch as one could love. The *prefident*, for example, whom we fup with
to-morrow, has nothing to recommend
him but his figure in the world; feventy
thoufand livres yearly rent, muft attone
for his other deficiencies. Setting afide his
table, he has nothing wherewith to entertain his friends, except fome old ftories
which you heard yefterday, and which
he cannot fail of telling in a manner a-
greeable enough, becaufe he has repeated
them a thoufand times over. The *marchionefs* whom I perceived treated you
with an extraordinary complaifance, I
dare fay has formed a defign upon your
heart: fhe is a woman indeed of a great
fortune; is feparated from a husband
whom fhe married meerly for love, yet

now hates to such a degree, as to allow him a confiderable penfion to leave her at liberty; as he has nothing of his own, and was never attached to her by inclination, he confented to part with her, and gives himfelf no pain concerning her conduct. She has already had three lovers, and I am much miftaken, if fhe does not intend you for the fourth. That gentleman who has engaged us for the third day, has a poft in the treafury: he does not want wit and politenefs it muft be confeft; but fuch a ridiculous affectation of being looked upon as a man of family, and that the employment he holds, is a difgrace to his birth, fpoils all his other good qualities, and makes him contemptible; fince it is well known he could not fupport the rank he holds, without that employment he feems to defpife. The lady who fat next to him, *purfued fhe with a very myfterious air*, is one whom it is neceffary I fhould particularly delineate to you, that you may not be deceived by that fhew of modefty fhe puts on. She was a poor orphan without any dowry, but her birth and beauty; I fhould have added her virtue, if fhe had maintained the fame opinion I had of her before her marriage.

marriage. A rich counsellor fell in love with her and made her his wife: he is a weak man and easily deceived. He permitted her to keep whatever company she thought fit, and she came frequently to my house, where I never perceived any insensibility in her to pleasure; however she all at once, gave over either visiting or being visited; she scarce ever goes out except to church, and even myself, who she has looked upon as her best friend, am sometimes three weeks without seeing her; I had the greatest difficulty imaginable to prevail on her to sup with me last night; but what do you think I have discovered within this month, she dies for the love of a young clerk of monsieur the counsellor, and it is to this minion she sacrifices her friends and her liberty.

As I had nothing to oppose against the pictures she drew of persons so little known to me, she went on in the same track: The fat abbey, *said she*, who was so facetious, has one of the best benefices in all *France*, and has besides a very great estate: yet even though his age would deny him all hope of posterity, if he had not renounced it by his profession, and has
none

none but very diſtant relations, of whom
he makes no account ; yet I am informed
by his domeſtics, that he burys his money. His friends, it is true, find ſomething to eat with him, but it is not often :
he does not enjoy one quarter of his revenue, which notwithſtanding, they ſay,
he makes an addition to by the meaneſt
methods : they tell me, *continued ſhe,
ſinking her voice*, that he lends out money upon pledges.

As to madam the *Counteſs*, who appeared ſo ſparkling, *purſued ſhe*, neither
wit nor beauty are wanting to render her
agreeable, and I know few women more
capable of friendſhip ; but her immoderate love of play has ruined her health,
and, I ſhould ſay, her fortune too, if one
of the commiſſioners of the treaſury did
not repair her loſſes. But did you take
notice, *cried ſhe, ſomewhat abruptly*, of
the *Maſter of Requeſts*, who ſat oppoſite
to you ? I know no one good quality that
he is not poſſeſt of, but am told for a certain truth, that he is but half a man, and
that hinders him from any thoughts of
marriage : his character, however, is
more ſupportable than that of the gentleman

tleman on your left hand : he has an infinity of wit, it is certain, and he has need of it, to engage me to suffer his visits ; for they say his taste of love is odious and ridiculous ; but it would not become a virtuous woman to speak on this occasion what it deserves.

IT would be too tedious to follow this lady through all her descriptions ; among the twelve persons who made the number of her guests, not one was spared ; and whatever idea she might give me of the characters of others, I could not be uncertain as to her own ; in painting them, she gave, without knowing it, an exact picture of herself ; and, without even suspecting her guilty of injustice, it was easy to discover, her soul was full of envy, dissimulation, and some sparks of cruelty ; otherwise the friendship she made professions of to each of these persons, would have rendered her more reserved as to their faults : but the reason of my remembering so particularly this conversation, will soon discover itself ; I regretted above all, that I had been deceived in the fair wife of the counsellor, whose virtue I imagined had been equal to her beauty.

A s

As the *President* was the firſt who had invited me to ſupper, I thought it would be expected, that I ſhould pay my reſpects to him before the time; accordingly I went, deſigning no more than to call at his houſe, juſt pay my compliments, or leave my name if he was abroad; the character I had heard of him, giving me no deſire of entring into any friendſhip with him; but I was much more happy than I deſerved: I found him at home, and was introduced to him in a fine library: I cannot believe, *ſaid he*, that the place I receive you in can be diſagreeable to you; perſons of all ages ought to have a taſte for reading, and for thoſe who think as I do, there cannot be ſo agreeable an avocation.

I was ſurprized to hear him ſpeak in this manner; however, as a fine collection of books is frequently owing to the affectation of the poſſeſſors, I knew not yet but he might aſſume an air of wiſdom, which would only ſerve to render his weakneſs more ridiculous: he continued to tell me, in the moſt eaſy manner, that his library was much leſs valuable to him

by

by the number, than by the choice of the
books it contained; that besides those
which appertained to his own science, he
had selected a few of the best writers on
every other, and to those he bounded his
application: I do not pretend, *said he,*
to that kind of learning which consists in
having read every thing, but in reading
those treatises from which I can receive
the greatest advantage, either as to the
improvement of my understanding, or my
morals.

I should pass my whole life entirely
here, *continued he,* if society did not
exact something from me, and was seldom out of it during the life of my wife,
to whom I left the care of doing the honours of my house; but have become more
communicative since her death; because
having a considerable fortune, I think I
ought not to live only for myself; but I
retain my former contempt of the world,
have so little taste for its frivolous amusements, its mistaken pursuits, miserable
morals, and for all that they call happiness and pleasure, that of all the places in
Paris, my own study is that which has
most charms for me. You comprehend

not

not the poſſibility of this, *continued he,
ſmiling* ; you are young, and to expect it
at your age, would be to contradict the
proverb ; however, I diſcovered ſo much
good ſenſe in you yeſterday, among an
aſſembly, where, perhaps, you were ſurprized to find ſo little, that I eaſily fore-
ſee you will ſooner or later come into my
way of thinking.

A diſcourſe ſo grave, and ſo judicious,
from the mouth of a perſon who had been
repreſented to me as a meer trifler, inſpired
me with a reſpect equal to my aſtoniſhment; but my admiration increaſed, when
having aſked me if I had any inclination
for the ſciences, he entered into a converſation on thoſe to which I had moſt applied myſelf: I could not here be deceived, becauſe having made a conſiderable
progreſs in them, the traces of which are
yet preſent with me, I was charmed to
hear him, with an incredible facility, not
only reaſon on all thoſe principles which
had been rendered familiar to me but by
the force of application, but open new
proſpects of knowledge to my comprehenſion, with a conſpicuity and ſtrength
exceeding all I had ever found in my moſt
ſkilful

skilful preceptors, or masters. I wish,
said he, after having finished his discourse,
that you may not reproach me for entertaining you in a manner so different from
the gaieties of last night, and in which,
in spite of my dislike, good manners o-
bliged me to take part.

Upon quitting him, with the most
profound veneration, I found little difficulty in comprehending, that a man of
such an extent of knowledge, should dis-
dain the frivolous subjects which are u-
sually the conversation of the table, or
that the superior turn of his genius should
indeed render him less capable of them,
than an infinity of superficial men and
women are; but I could not conceive
how women, and many men, who did
not think more justly, or could reason
on better principles than they, should
presume to set up for judges of merit,
and arbitrers of reputation. The *President*, who had the true qualities of wit,
with all the improvements of learning,
out of meer complaisance sometimes took
part in those frivolous amusements that
engage the most of people, which, not
being able to execute with all the vivacity

city expected from him, and is indeed
necessary to render folly pleasing, those
whom his justice would have made him
despise, turned the tables upon him, and
robbed him of that respect which was
his due. I could not presently discover
from what source this want of judgment,
even in persons of condition, proceeded:
it must certainly be, *said I, to myself,* either that nature bestows that gift on very
few, or that the greatest number lose its
use for want of cultivation, and by a habitude of light and trifling chimeras : this
last it was which I found the most probable cause. Thus a certain liveliness
passes for wit, and that positiveness in
asserting, which the vanity of birth or
fortune inspires, is frequently mistaken
for solid understanding, especially when
enforced by a facility of utterance (which
is no more than a mechanical advantage,
dependant on memory, practice, and the
organs of speech,) which, with some o-
ther qualities of the same kind, such as
the example of others, the custom of the
world, and the desire of being applauded,
are easily acquired. Thus, with no
trouble or expence of thought, are our
fashionable judges enabled to cry down
all

all who are not like themſelves ; and to turn into ridicule that true merit, which, if they took the pains to examine, would ſerve to confound and humble them.

I did not, however, indulge theſe reflections for any length of time : after leaving the *Preſident*, I bethought myſelf of waiting on Monſieur the *Marſhal de V****, who, I knew, had received a letter from my father in my favour : for that end, I went firſt to the *Marquiſs de * * **, an intimate of my father's, and had been a field-marſhal as well as himſelf ; and on my deſiring him to introduce me to the palace of *V****, he aſked me, with what views I intended to addreſs him ? On which I naturally told him, my hopes were to procure a troop of horſe, that I might be in the way of obtaining a regiment whenever a war ſhould happen. You are in the right, *anſwered he*, your age and your birth require your entering into the ſervice ; but when you have paſſed five and thirty, or forty years, as I have done in it, I wiſh you may leave it more rich, and more happy. I have waſted my whole

whole fortune, and, at the age you fee me, have nothing remaining but a title, and fome fcars. I regret not, however, *added he*, that I have obeyed the calls of honour, though the diforder of my affairs obliges me to have frequent recourfe to a relation who has a poft in the treafury, and does not think himfelf demeaned by a poffeffion which has made his fortune in the world. On his mentioning the name of this gentleman, I knew it was the fame I had fupped with at the houfe of the *Intendant*'s lady, and whom fhe had reprefented in colours fo contemptible. How, *faid I*, is Monfieur * * * of your kindred? They have not that idea of him in the world. I know not what they may think of his birth, *replyed he*, but his grand-father was the brother of mine, and by confequence he is of as good a family as I am. I was not lefs furprifed at this difcovery, than I had been concerning the *Prefident*. Thus *faid I to myfelf*, one may be ignorant what a perfon is, with whom one is moft familiar. But how bafe is it to imagine the worft? and to propagate that imagination as a reality, by averring to others, what we know nothing

thing of ourfelves, and if we pleafed might be better informed.

WE went towards evening to the palace of *V*****, where we found the marfhal engaged at play, but that did not hinder him from receiving me with the utmoft politenefs. I had not time however, to enter into any particulars with him, becaufe of the great number of perfons who were no more than fpectators of the diverfion he and fome others were taken, and who came one after another, when they had learned my name to pay their compliments, the moft of them being officers of diftinction who had ferved with my father. The *Count de ****** then colonel of the king's dragoons, interefted himfelf fo far in the defign I had of buying a company, that he propofed my accepting one in his regiment, which was going to be vacant by the retreat of an ancient captain, who had obtained permiffion to difpofe of his commiffion. I agreed to this propofal without hefitation, and the bargain was immediately concluded between us. Monfieur the marfhal who foon heard what I had done, reproached my precipitation, and complained to the *Count* that he had difap

pointed

pointed the designs he had for me. My father's letter having intimated a desire of my serving under his son who was also a colonel, though not of dragoons; I was sensible that would have cost me much less; but the fidelity owing to my word, would not suffer me to break the engagement I had already entered into; and thus I became all at once, and without thinking of it a moment before, in possession of a title, to which I could not have so soon aspired.

MONSIEUR the marshal having with a great deal of goodness, entreated me to regard his house as that of my father, it was natural for me to stay supper; but before the hour arrived, one of my servants called me into the anti-chamber, and told me that a person from my country waited at home to speak with me, having rode post to communicate to me some very important affairs he was charged with. A sudden alarm for the health of my father made me immediately depart, and I found a man whom I knew to be of the same province, but was not acquainted with him. Af-

C   ter

ter he had put a letter into my hands, he told me without informing me from whom it came, or giving me time to examine the contents, that I might confide entirely in him, and honour him with my commands ; that he knew the fecret of my heart, and was devoted to my fervice, and fhould expect, nor defire no other recompence than my friendfhip. A difcourfe fo obfcure, made me look firft on the name fubfcribed at the bottom of the letter, and found it that of madamoifelle *de S. V***** the lady whom I had teftified fome little regard for before I left the country, and who unknown to me had been the defigned bride of my father. I could not guefs on what account I received this favour from her, but hafted to inform myfelf by reading what fhe had wrote. After fome fhort prelude, fhe told me my precipitate departure had given her more grief, than aftonifhment ; that fhe could not believe a perfon who had given her fo much caufe to think that he loved her, could ever be brought to treat her with indifference ; that to do juftice to my character, fhe muft impute my

flight

flight to the orders of a jealous father,
who had long loved, and had since offered her his hand ; but that having
made me the master of her heart, she had
rejected a proposal so injurious to my
hopes ; gave repeated assurances never
to bestow herself on any other than myself, and concluded with telling me, she
had taken a resolution to follow me, in
order to be united for ever ; and had sent
a person in whom she could confide to
apprize me of it, and to whom she
begged I would discover the sincerity of
my intentions concerning her.

SURE never was any astonishment
equal to mine after reading this epistle :
I had often seen the lady, had behaved
to her with the regard due to her sex
and rank ; and 'tis possible with somewhat more than at that time I should
have paid to any other, who might have
been her equal. I know not but the ardour
of youth, and the idle life I led while
in the country, might in time have kindled in me a real passion for her ; but I
never made the least declaration to her of
any sentiments of that kind, much less

had

had entertained the leaſt thought of marriage, my head and heart being wholly
taken up with other views. I recollected in my mind every paſſage of the little converſation I had with her, but
could find none that could give her room
to believe herſelf the object of my wiſh-
es, or occaſion any in her, which ſhould
inſpire her with ſo wild a reſolution, as
that of following me. In conſidering her
character, ſhe appeared a woman to
whom I ſhould never have been ſeriouſly
attached, having always obſerved in her,
a much greater ſhare of vivacity, than
ſolidity ; but had it been otherwiſe, I
ſhould have thought it little becoming
in me, to diſpute her with my father.
After ſome reflections on the oddneſs of
the circumſtance, I found the danger of
deferring one moment the undeceiving
her ; and as I took leſs pleaſure than the
greateſt part of my ſex and age, in tri-
umphing over a heart, to which I had
no pretenſions : I determined to anſwer
her letter immediately, but in a ſtile leſs
gallant, than honeſt and ſincere, in order to diſſipate thoſe falſe ideas ſhe had
conceived of me.

I

I declared my mind to her confident, who feemed in the utmoft confternati-on; perhaps Monfieur, *faid he*, you do not know that your father has affured her of all he fhall die poffeffed of. No, *replyed I*, but I know that I fhall be glad fhe makes him happy on that conditi-on. I then fat down to write in the man-ner I had refolved; and when I had finifhed, defired the man to return to her with it; and that he would fet out on his journey the fame night.

THIS adventure, though I was far from forefeeing the confequences, put me enough out of humour to keep me at home the following day; I know not whether, through the apprehenfions of occafioning fome anxiety to my father, on the account of his paffion, or, that of his fufpecting me of an attempt, to break off his marriage, from a felf-in-terrefted view. I went, however, to fup with the *Prefident*, as I had promifed, and found there the *Intendant*'s lady, with feveral of thofe, I had feen at her houfe, and others, altogether unknown

to

to me. Our worthy hoft, appeared with more chearfulnefs, than I had feen him before; but the fimplicity of his dif-courfe, and manners, was the fame. I doubted not, but many of his guefts, thought they did him a favour, to liften to him fometimes, though far from fet-ting any value on that fund of know-ledge he was mafter of, he defcended to enter into the torrent of their idle chat, to avoid giving any one pain, by fhewing the wide difference between his underftanding and theirs: he did, in-deed, mingle fome old ftories, as the *Intendant*'s lady had obferved, and told them in a very agreeable manner, but he could rarely finifh without being in-terrupted by one or other of the com-pany, who feemed impatient to relate fome fcandalous aneƈdote, or criticifm on the play aƈted that day. The *Marchionefs*, with three lovers, and the coun-fellor's young wife, having excufed them-felves from accepting the invitation made to them, the moft malicious motives were affigned for their ftaying at home, and having once begun upon each, ap-peared to vie with the other which fhould

be

be moſt ſevere, or moſt witty, as they imagined, on the real or ſuppoſed frailties of theſe two abſent ladies. They were too little known to me, for me to urge any thing in their vindication ; but though my attention was awakened on the name of the counſellor's wife, yet I was leſs concerned in her innocence, than I was to hear perſons, who pretended to wit and good breeding, treat in ſo ſcandalous a manner an amiable woman, who could not loſe all her merit by having given way to a capricious paſſion. Happening, at laſt, to mention the *Financier*, who likewiſe was not there, I ſuppoſe, *ſaid one of the gentlemen*, he is taken up with finding out ſome new titles appertaining to his family,——which he will tell us of the next time he does us the honour to come among us, replied another. This raillery appeared ſo ſhocking to me, after the account the *Marquiſs* had given me, that I had not the power to forbear attempting to undeceive them : I know Monſieur *de* * * *, but of yeſterday, *interrupted I,* yet if you have any doubt of his birth, I can aſſure you he is of

the

the houfe of * * *, and a near kinfman
to the *Marquifs* of that name ; in fpite
of the civilities they had always fhewn
me, they could not hear thefe words
without joining in an immoderate laughter, in the midft of which the *Intendant*'s lady cried, fure you have forgot
what I told you yefterday ? Monfieur,
the Count, is but juft arrived here, *rejoined another*, and we ought not to be
furprized to find him ignorant of thefe
things. No, no, *cried one of the long
robe*, it is we ourfelves, who do not enter into the irony of *Monfieur* the
Count's expreffion ; did he not fay, he
knew him but of yefterday ? what is a
man of yefterday ? is he not a man who
ftands in need of a title ? perhaps the
Financier might purchafe one yefterday
at the houfe of * * *, for I think the
head of it is not very eafy in his fortune.

On this, a fecond fhout arofe among
them, and I muft confefs, this torrent of
impertinence and ill-nature excited in
me fome fparks of indignation. Wit is
very enchanting, *faid I*, but it ought
not to be exercifed at the expence of
                                    truth

truth and juſtice; I flatter myſelf that I may be believed on my word: I yeſter-day ſaw the Marquiſs *de* * * *, who is an antient friend of my father; he told me, I know not on what occaſion, that the grand-father of Monſieur the *Finan-cier*, and his, were brothers, which certainly makes him and the Marquiſs cou-ſin-germans. The ſerious and reſolute air with which I accompanied theſe words, prevented any reply being immediately given to them; but did not put an entire ſtop to their ſeverities af-terwards. Monſieur the *Count* has been in *Paris* but two days, *ſaid one*, and may eaſily be deceived by a parity of names. Who knows after all, *rejoined another*, but the Marquiſs *de* * * * may be paid for owning a new kinſman, we all know he is not rich. Thus they con-tinued till the *Preſident* put an end to the ſcene, by ſaying that he did not know the origin of Monſieur * * *, but he knew that *Paris* was full of ſcan-dal and detraction, and little regard was to be paid to the moſt current reports.

AFTER the company broke up, I fell again into my former reflections, and made a resolution never to judge of any person by the character bestowed on them by the world.

I cannot nevertheless deny, but these people, in whom I had discovered so much lightness and injustice, had some qualities I thought amiable enough, but at the same time knew they were only such as flattered my taft for pleasure: my cooler reason could not approve that truth and decency should become the sacrifice of wit, and the sallies of imagination: vivacity could not compensate for want of sincerity; and too great a penetration, seemed to denote the heart of the quick-sighted, into the faults of others not altogether innocent itself. In a word, the sprightly repartees, and lively expressions which engaged my ear; the beauty of the women, and graceful behaviour of the men which charmed my eye, and the luxury of the table which gratified my palate, were all insufficient to attone for other qualities, which could not be ascribed to this assembly,

sembly, and my mind found nothing
worthy of delighting itself with, on recollecting what had past at these two
entertainments.

HOWEVER, that I might not fall
myself into the same error I condemned,
by judging others by this essay, I proceeded the following days to fulfill all the
engagements I had made. Though the
greatest part of the company I saw at
every one of these houses were still the
same ; yet they were always intermixed
with new faces, which gave me the occasion of encreasing my acquaintance
very largely. Several there were whom
at first sight, I took to be persons of
sense and solidity; the company being
generally engaged before supper at various games of cards, and that diversion
allowed no opportunity of knowing
them better, and if any time remained
between that and sitting down to table,
the conversation was bounded between
those who had been of the same party
at play ; so that I could form no deci-
sive judgment on the characters of those
who were strangers. But no sooner was

the

the entertainment ferved up, than I perceived the difference between my old
and new acquaintance could not be diftinguifhed; thofe whofe memory and
imagination had appeared leaft awake, I
now found waited but for the cue, thofe
of more warm ideas gave to be as loud,
and as impertinent as they.

I was not all this while neglectful of
my affairs, I concluded that I had with
Monfieur the *Count de C* * * * concerning
my company, as I had no great inclination to join the regiment, which was
garrifoned at *Sedan*, he told me, I might
wait till it came to *Paris*, as he expected it would in about three months.

I dined frequently at the palace of
V * *, and the *Marfhal* being always
accompanied by a great number of experienced officers, I had the means of
improving myfelf by their difcourfes,
in the fcience I had embraced. But
though there was nothing of aufterity in
the behaviour, either of the *Marfhal*,
or his guefts, yet I found not in their
converfation, thofe pleafures which were
                                        agree-

agreeable to my age and inclination, a-
ny more than I did those capable of
entertaining my reason and understanding, in the companies with whom I had
supped.

THE old *Marquiſs de* * * * whom
I saw frequently, and from whom I expected to receive many instructions;
asked me one day where, and in what
manner I paſt my evenings; on which
I gave him a detail of those engagements, which had taken me up since
my arrival. He knew several of those
who viſited the *Intendant*'s lady, particularly, the commander of * * *, who,
he told me, was his intimate friend. After giving that gentleman some part of
the praiſes, which were indeed his due,
he added, that with all his good qualities, riches and figure, he was the man
of the whole world moſt deſerving com-
miſeration: I have known him long,
ſaid he, but never knew his infirmities till within theſe two months.——I
went to viſit him one morning, and
entring familiarly into his chamber, ſurprized him between the hands of his
Valet de Chambre, who was wrapping
him

him up in an infinite number of band-
ages: he then made no fcruple of re-
vealing to me, that fince fifteen years
of age he had been afflicted with a terrible diforder, which had obliged him
to enter into the order of *Malta*, which
enforces continence.   How, *cried I*,
the world imputes his coldnefs for the
women to another caufe.   I tell you the
truth, *replied·the Marquifs*, but he does
not chufe it fhould be fpoke of, and
perhaps I am guilty of an indifcretion
in acquainting you with it.   I then repeated to him what I had heard from
the *Intendant*'s lady, and other women ;
on which he put on a fmile, which had
fomewhat of malice in it.   For my part,
I found nothing but new proofs of the
falfity of public judgments; but as it
was not on the fubject of morality,
that I wanted to hear the *Marquifs*
fpeak, I faid no more to him on this
matter.   He reproached me for having
confined myfelf fo much to one focie·
ty, when there were numbers in *Paris* to afford variety of amufement:----
This city, *faid he*, has wherewith to
fatisfy all kinds of taftes: every quarter

ter abounds with houses where you
have a right to go as often as you please,
after having been once introduced. The
persons who keep them are of condition, you will sometimes find good
company there, and always good wine
and eating; much the same as that of
madam the *Intendant*'s lady, and others
you have mentioned; but in those, though
you meet with an infinite deal of wit
and pleasantry, yet it is an irregular sort
of wit and pleasantry, from which you
reap no fruits. But there are other societies, *continued he, with an unusual
sparkle in his eyes,* which I prefer to all
the rest: —— Societies composed of
persons, who know how to make the
most of life, by uniting all the different
pleasures it can give. Persons, who are
all devoted to the same passion, converse
together without ceremony; and are under no concern for what others do, nor
for what may be said of themselves. If
you look into the world, you will find
no happiness among those assemblies,
which have different inclinations; the
great drinkers, associate themselves with
those who are so; the learned, seek the
conversation

converfation of men of letters; the religious, are only eafy with the religious ;
and the libertine, cannot enjoy himfelf,
without the company of thofe, who
are of his own way of thinking. As
for me, I am for thofe parties of pleafure I have mentioned, and pafs moft
of my nights in them. What think
you Monfieur, *added he*, will you make
one among us this evening?

THOUGH I could not fee much to
approve, in that propenfity to pleafure,
in a man of the marquifs's age ; yet, the
juft defcription he had given of that fociety, of which the *Intendant*'s lady
was the head, made me have a better
idea of this he recommended to me;
and I fhould have immediately accepted
his offer, if I had not been previoufly
engaged.

I had feen the counfellor's wife but
once, and being furprized that fhe had
never been at any of the fuppers fince
I mentioned it to the *Intendant*'s lady
with an eagernefs, which drew fome
raillery upon me; fhe afked me if I intended

tended to fupplant the young clerk, and
as I had been a little angry with my
heart, for receiving any impreffions in
favour of a woman, faid to be capable
of fo unworthy an attachment, I made
no difficulty in replying, that I had no
ambition, of following fuch a general
as *Medor*, for I had heard, that was
the name of the young clerk. However, I expreffed a defire of feeing her
again, on which the lady told me, that
after refufing a great many invitations, fhe
had prevailed on her, to fup at her houfe
that fame night. --- Is it not a great
honour to me, *cried fhe laughing*, to
be preferred this once to her *Medor?*

It was on this account, I defired the
Marquifs, to remit my going to the
company he fpoke of, till another time;
on which he told me, he regretted the
pleafure I deprived myfelf of; but added, that I might come at the hour, I
fhould find myfelf at liberty, for they
never feparated till morning, and he
would acquaint them beforehand, of
the gueft, they were to expect. ---- I
then, gave him my promife to go, and
                                    wrote

wrote down in my table a direction to
the place

From him, I went to the *Intendant*'s lady: ſhe had already, a great
deal of company with her; and the
parties for play, were ſetled. ------- She
made a ſign for me to come near, and
ſaid in my ear, I ſhall fall into diſgrace
with you; the lady, has been ſo cruel
to ſend me word, ſhe has impoſed it
as a law upon herſelf, not to ſup abroad.
I know not to what you will attribute this refuſal: but, I do not wonder at it, *added ſhe, with a moſt malicious
tone*, and ſhall rejoyce at the happineſs
of *Medor*. I made a ſuitable anſwer,
to theſe words, though it was rather
to diſguiſe the vexation, this diſappoint-
ment gave me, than that my heart approved of what ſhe ſaid. The aſſembly
being very numerous, without me, I
thought, in a houſe where I ſo often
ſupped, I was under no neceſſity of
conſtraining myſelf; and the party, the
Marquiſs mentioned to me, running in
my head, I went away without being
taken notice of, and order'd my coach,
                       which

which waited in the court-yard, to drive
where he had appointed.

I had known no more of the *Marquifs*, till my arrival at *Paris*, than his
name; that he was a friend of my father's, had ferved with honour, and
had fpent the beft part of his fortune;
but the little time I had converfed with
him, fhewed much more of his character. As I vifited him chiefly, in the hope
of improving my knowledge, in military
affairs; I heard him fpeak on that topic, with a fatisfaction which made me
truly love him: ---- the inclination he
had this day, teftified for pleafure, did
not much furprize me; but, I could
not help admiring that vivacity, which,
at his age enabled him to purfue it. The
picture he had given, of what I was to
expect where I was going, filled me
with impatience. ---- Mufic, dancing,
beautiful women, men of fpirit and politenefs; the moft delicate chear, and excellent wine, feemed to me to be the re-
quifites of uniting all the pleafures of
life; and thefe I doubted not to find. The
door was no fooner opened, than I faw
the

the *Marquifs* running to meet me, with
the utmoft fatisfaction ; --- come, *faid
he*, I have told them of you, --- you
are expected and wifhed for.   He then
acquainted me with the names of the
perfons ; who were all men of birth,
and diftinguifhed merit.

I was conducted into an apartment,
which, though not very fpacious, by
its elegance, and propriety, confirmed
the character had been given me, of
thofe who frequented it --- The richnefs
of the furniture, was the leaft to be
praifed in it; but nothing for eafe,
pleafure, and convenience, were wanting : all was illuminated, with a prodi-
gious number of wax candles; from
this, we paffed into a drawing-room,
where the company were feated, but
rofe to receive me. ---- I was prefented to the owner of this agreeable recefs; who advanced to meet me
with an eafy and polite civility; on cafting my eyes on one fide the room, I faw
three ladies of a very beautiful appearance, to whom I hafted with a profound reverence : they were dreft with
the

the utmoſt exactneſs, had ſomewhat of
an uncommon gracefulneſs in their air,
and ſeemed no way diſcompoſed at the
ſight of a ſtranger.   After this I turned
to the gentlemen, and the ceremonies
between our ſex being ſhort, we all ſat
down.----I was about to relate the occaſion which procured me the pleaſure of
coming ſome hours before I expected,
when I was interrupted by the old *Marquiſs*, who taking hold of one of the
ladies, cried, *Fanchon!* why doſt not
thou embrace *Monſieur* the *Count?* on
which ſhe roſe and did as he deſired,
though with an air of modeſty enough:
and thou *Liſetta!* and thou *Catin! ſaid
he to the other two*, muſt alſo do the
ſame.   They were no leſs complying,
than the former had been, and each in
her turn took me in her arms.

I muſt confeſs, that in my firſt ſur-
prize at a civility ſo ſtrange and unlook-
ed for, I received it with ſome tokens of
confuſion: I had imagined that the *Chevalier* had given an entertainment to
ſome of his friends, and their peculiar
miſtreſſes; and the familiarity with
which

which I found the *Marquiſs* treated them, I thought his character, as an old man, and a ſoldier, might ſometimes authorize him to be a little forgetful of the decorum due to the ſex ; but this laſt compliment he made me, opened the ſcene to my comprehenſion ; and as they doubtleſs looked upon me as a novice in the cuſtoms of ſociety, this was a ſignal to inſtruct me.----Now all reſerve was thrown aſide.----One threw himſelf at his length on a couch, another lolled upon a carpet ; a third took *Fanchon* and led her round the room in a minuet ſtep ; a fourth began to ruffle the other women, and to pull off their tippets and mantelets, in order, *as he ſaid*, to diſplay more of their charms---The *Marquiſs* told me they were juſt come upon the town, that this was the ſecond party they had made, and that their beauty had been ſo much celebrated, ſince an entertainment made for them two days before, by *Monſieur* the duke *de* * * *, that theſe gentlemen had promiſed each of them five *Lewis-d'ors*, to engage them to come that evening.

FOR

FOR my part, I kept my feat till the *Marquifs* obliging me to pluck off my fword, whifpered in my ear, the girls are fafe, *faid he*, we can anfwer for their health; and you may have your choice, therefore make no fcruple of following your inclinations. It was eafy for me to underftand what he meant; but having refolved to keep myfelf within bounds, I only confidered how to behave, fo as to be agreeable in this company without engaging too far.— I faw moft of the gentlemen difappear fucceffively, with one or other of the women; but they did not abfent themfelves for any long time, and each thought on the neceffities of others, in fatisfying his own. The *Chevalier de* * * * who was the owner of the houfe, feeing fo little ardour in me to take my turn, began to rally me upon it; on which I excufed myfelf, by pretending I had been with much the fame fort of company. the night before.----Liberty, *faid he*, liberty is the golden age; but we fhall find ways to make you recover your forces. ---- As I faw the leaft referve

would

would render me ridiculous; I laughed,
I fung, I danced, and in fine, gave
into all the fooleries of the fociety. I
found indeed, that the manner in which
they behaved, had charms for thofe of
all ages, who had abandoned themfelves to libertinifm ; and that even fuch
as the *Marquifs* might procure for his
money, thofe pleafures which he could
not hope for by ways more gallant and
honourable; but thefe kind of amours
had in them fomewhat too grofs for me.
This common communication difgufted
me, and I was aftonifhed to find any
young man who did not want accomplifh-
ments, worthy of acquiring him a more
delicate intercourfe, could have the leaft
relifh for an object, whom he faw the
moment before come out of the arms of
another.----I was falling into thefe reflections, when the *Marquifs* cried to
me, is not this the true happinefs of life?
For my part, I know no other, and never regret parting with my money for
the purchafe of it. I replied, that he
was very fortunate to be able to purchafe happinefs, at the rate of a few
crowns. But I faw by this confeffion,
                                    the

the true cause of the ruin of his estate;
and judged by him that many of those
officers whose affairs were in a bad condition after their quitting the service,
ought not to lay the blame of their misfortunes on the occupation they had
been in.

IN spite of the little regard, it was
natural for me to have for three creatures who made so unworthy a use of
their charms; I could not forbear feeling a certain compassion for their age,
and the poverty which had perhaps obliged them to abandon all sense of shame
or principle: the eldest of them not exceeding seventeen : *Fanchon* above all
inspired me with so lively a pity, that
I fell into the most serious reflections on
the injustice of fortune : besides the re-
gularity of her features, and the delicacy of her complection; there was
something so noble, and so modest in
her air, that had I seen her at church,
or at court, I should have taken her for
a maid of the first quality----Is it not a
melancholy thing, *said I to myself*, that
this unhappy creature, who has beauty

D enough

enough to make a worthy man happy
in her poſſeſſion, and to fix herſelf in
an honourable condition, ſhould be de-
ſtined to paſs her youth in the moſt infamous diſſolution? while I was taken
up with this thought, my eyes were
fixed intently on her, and ſhe imagined
that being the only one who had not retired, either with her, or her companions, I was now beginning to feel
ſome amorous emotions in her favour;
and the *Marquiſs* and *Chevalier*, having
charged her to omit nothing that might
awaken my deſires, ſhe ſtarted from her
ſeat, and came running to me with o-
pen arms. This action gave me the
opportunity of putting in execution a
deſign I had juſt then formed: I returned
her carreſſes with the appearance of an
equal warmth; and withdrew with her
into an adjacent chamber; all the company claped their hands, applauding the vi-
ctory ſhe ſeemed to have gained over my
coldneſs, and I left them to indulge that
opinion.

Being alone with her, after having
locked the door, I made her ſit down
in an eaſy chair, and placing myſelf near
her;

her; you are charming, *said I in the most tender accent*, I know no woman more beautiful; but before I proceed any farther with you, I would willingly know, how long it is since you have taken up this course of life, and if you find any real satisfaction in it? to which *she replied*, that she had been in public no more than two days; and as to my other demand, confessed that she was pleased with seeing such noblemen as I was. O! *said I*, you cannot persuade me, that yesterday was your first essay; and to put you out of pain, I declare to you that your dealing sincerely with me in this article, will make no alteration in my sentiments, because I have no design to partake your favours: yet I shall nevertheless make you a present of some *Lewis d'res*; but I insist on your telling the truth, *continued I*, and above all, whether you take pleasure in this infamous life. This term, which escaped me perhaps too soon, seemed to dispose her to speak more freely, but she added to the former assurances she had given me many asseverations, that this was the second day of her libertinism, and then told me a long story of her having been

debauched

debauched by a *Major* of horfe, who
having brought her from her parents,
dyed without having made the fettle-
ment on her he had promifed ; and that
not daring to return to her kindred, fhe
had accepted an offer made by a woman
of her acquaintance, who told her fhe
would fupport her in a handfome manner, if fhe confented to yield herfelf to
the pleafures of young gentlemen. In
regard to any fatisfaction I find in it, *faid*
fhe, you may judge, that a young perfon
brought up to different expectations,
muft have fufficient caufe to lament the
fad neceffity, which has reduced her to
fo fhameful an expedient. Some tears
which fell from her eyes in fpeaking
thefe laft words, perfectly convinced me
of the truth of them, and that fhe indeed regretted the fituation fhe was in.--
I expreffed no curiofity of knowing her
birth, but promifed to ferve her, if fhe
quitted her prefent debaucheries. O ! *cri-*
ed fhe, lifting up her hands and eyes, it
is all the bleffing I defire of heaven.---
I fhould be too happy in finding a worthy gentleman to take care of me. Perceiving fhe did not comprehend my
meaning

meaning, I explained it. To take care of you, *said I*, is to put you in a condition to live honestly by the work of your hands.---This is the offer I make you, and shall perform it with pleasure ; but it is not my inclination to engage with you any otherwise. Though this explication was far from answering her first idea of me, yet she appeared highly satisfied with it, and her gratitude carried her so far as to kiss my hands, and wet them with her tears. I then took directions where she might be found, and having assured her, that she should hear from me very soon, gave her four *Lewis d'ores*, as an earnest of what I intended to do for her. After which we returned to the company, who imagined we had been taken up by a quite different entertainment.

EVERY one congratulated *Fanchon* on the power of her charms ; she received their compliments as her due, and I did not disown that she had cause. However, as I foresaw she would be exposed to many other attacks in the course of a long night, it came in my

D 3   head

head to preferve her from them, by making ufe of an innocent deception : I whifpered to the *Marquifs* and fome others, that I had fome reafons not to be perfectly fatisfied as to my health, and that was the caufe that I took *Fanchon* out the laft, as fearing to do an injury to any of the company : this falfe confidence was immediately fpread among all the men, and fucceeded perhaps too well for the inclinations of *Fanchon*, who was treated the reft of the night as a veftal.

The hour of fupper being arrived, we feated ourfelves at table, which was ferved with the utmoft variety and elegance ; and this was the only part of the entertainment, in which I found nothing difagreeable ; the converfation was fo eafy, and withal fo fpirituous, that I rejoiced to find it take a turn, in which I could bear a part, without prejudice to my principles or underftanding. It was not indeed on things profounded we difcourfed: they would have appeared unfeafonable in a party of pleafure ; but there is a manner of making the moft trifling

subjects

subjects afford some improvement, as well as delight.--The sallies of wit went no farther than to heighten innocent mirth, and never launched out into injustice or detraction, on the character of any absent person. In fine, it was such as proved good nature and wit, are not things incompatible, and that the most lively gaiety has no occasion to transgress the bounds of decency. But my mind had no sooner began to give this behaviour all the applause it merited, when the women who had all this time being taken up with eating and drinking, now gave their tongues a loose, and a reverse of all had been so pleasing to me presently ensued, an inundation of impertinence and scandal, broke down all the dams of good breeding to those present, and consideration of the absent.---Neither age, nor sex, nor rank were spared; it was sufficient to be known to be ridiculed, or censured: intrigues were ascribed to every fine woman, and every husband laughed at for his blindness, or his imbecillity. My recent arrival at *Paris* excused me from entring into these details; and I observed

ferved to the *Chevalier*, that the room
was full of fervants, who liftned to all
was faid with the greateft attentive. It
is very true, *replied he*, but one is apt to
forget thefe things.—He then called for
the defert, which being brought, and
the table filled with *Champaign*, *Bur-
gundy*, *Greek* wines, and all forts of liquors, he ordered the footmen to leave
the room, and fhut the door.

I was in hopes, that in this interval,
fome other fubjects of difcourfe might
be ftarted; nor was I deceiv'd: after
having made fome encomiums, on the
excellence of the wine, they became
more ferious; and by degrees, fell upon the principles of religion. --- I forbear to repeat the thoufand little cavils,
which the fophiftry of infidelity made ufe
of; but, with regret I fpeak it; among all
the company, *Chriftianity* found not
one defender: and, the moft moderate were thofe, who reduced all
faith, to the acknowledging a *Deity:*
I began, with more zeal than prudence,
to combat fome of thofe arguments,
which I thought I might confute, without

out feeming to pique myfelf, on a fu-
perior judgment: but I foon perceived,
they were all of them perfons, who,
wanted not to be convinced; and having taken it into their heads, to difbe-
lieve every thing; made not their objections, with a defire of having them
refolved. The *Marquifs*, aftonifhed to
hear me fpeak, in a manner, fo different
from the others; afked me, whether, I
was going to turn *Apoftle*, and how I
came on a fudden, to be poffeft of fuch
a fpirit of devotion; which, he had
never known me in before? As to devotion, *anfwered I*, I have too little,
and ought to reproach myfelf, for being
fo far out of my duty; but I have the
extremeft honour for religion; and fhall
always declare I have fo, even before
thofe, who feem to renounce it. This
was perhaps, fomething more than is required of me; but I could not anfwer
to myfelf, the falfifying the dictates of
my heart; which, makes me believe,
there are more real Atheifts, than one
thinks for. To imagine, all thofe, who
affect to be fo, are otherwife; would
be, according to my opinion, giving
them a more contemptible character.

THOUGH, the manner in which I
ſpoke this, had nothing ſhocking in it;
yet, the *Marquiſs*, took an occaſion of
breaking off a diſcourſe, which was
much leſs agreeable to him, than the
new pleaſures he propoſed: he reminded us, that the night was far ſpent, and
we ought to make the moſt of what remained.   Then, taking the women,
who by this time, were half overcome
with wine, and drouzineſs, into the
next room; and deſiring us to follow
him, prepared for us, a new ſcene of
diverſion: which was this.   He pluck-
ed the matraſs from the couch, the
cuſhions from the chairs, and the carpet from the table; and ſpread them on
the floor: and then, told the women,
they would not ſupport their character,
if they did not play ſome pretty
tricks on the Stage, he had provided
for them.   All novices, as they had
pretended, I found they were no
ſtrangers to what he meant: *Fanchon*,
however, whom the wine had not made
forgetful of the engagement ſhe had
entered into with me; gave me a look,
which

which seemed to demand my consent;
but the *Marquiss*, that same instant,
throwing her down, with the rest of
her companions, the sport began; and
these miserable creatures, shewed their a-
gility, at the hazard of their necks;
tumbling heels over head, so fast, that
I was astonished they could hold it out.
I was witness for about a quarter of an
hour of this ridiculous spectacle, but
when they proceeded to postures yet
more indecent, I had much ado to conceal my disgust: turning my head, I
saw a glimpse of light at the corner of
a distant window, which made me
know it was broad-day, on which I
went under the curtain, and opened
the shutter. This window commanded a fine garden, which I had not seen
before, and the freshness of the morning, the sweetness of the air, and the
beautifulness of the prospect was so
transporting to me, that I fancied myself in another world. Looking on my
watch, I found it was near five o'clock,
and we were in the month of *May*,
which at *Paris*, is the most delightful
season of the year.----My breast and

head,

head, which had both been oppreſſed
by the heat of the apartment, and the
vapour of the wines, were inexpreſſibly
comforted by this freedom of reſpiration.   On obſerving more attentively
the beauties of this garden, I found that
in a ſmall ſpace of ground, a thouſand
charms were aſſembled : the parterres
were cut out with the utmoſt elegance,
and the graſs plats bordered with an infinite variety of flowers; a wall on each
ſide covered with lawrel, fillaree and
other ever-greens, bounded the proſpect
on the right and left, for a ſmall ſpace;
then ſpread and diſcovered four ſquares
ornamented with ſtatues.   I did not examine whether they were taken from hiſtory or fable, but the art of the carver
was excellent, eſpecially in the nuditi-
es.   Beyond this was a larger graſs plat,
of a ſemi-circular form, edged with
thick ſhrubs in bloſſom, and about two
foot in height.   Here were a groupe of
other ſtatues in different attitudes; ſome
ſtanding, others ſtooping, others ſitting,
according to the imagination of the ma-
ker: they were nymphs, demy-gods
and cupids.   Two large alleys went to
the

the extremity of the garden, and led to
a small, but very thick wood, where
were an infinite number of narrow paths
which all conducted to some agreeable
point ; but the two great walks which
still continued, ended at the entrance
of two grotto's, ornamented with rock-
work and painting : in a word, there
was nothing wanting but *cascades*, to
have rendered this the most delicious
retreat in the universe.

I was beginning to re-examine all the
beauties I saw before me, when I perceived
the *Marquis* come out in such a diforder, that he was scarce to be known :
his perriwig on one side, his linnen dir-
ty, his cloaths unbuttoned, staggering
as he went, and his leggs ready to sink
under the weight of his body ; but my
shock encreased, as he came nearer, and
I found his face of a deadly paleness ;
his eyes sunk in his head, and his lips
of a livid blew. The others appeared
successively, and were in much the same
condition.----What a spectacle would
this have been to a man entirely sober !
even I, who had my brain much disor-
dered

dered with the strength of the liquors, and want of sleep; had yet remains enough of reason, to compare the different objects before me.----On the one hand, I beheld nature animated in all her productions; the sun was beginning to send forth his radiance; the flowers opened themselves, and discovered the most smiling colours: various kinds of birds united in a melodious concert; and a triumphant splendor sat on the bough of every tree.----On the other side, I saw in my companions all the marks of languor and decay: they were disfigured, withered, their features lengthened, their spirits exhausted, and both mind and body enervated and weakned.----They wanted a dark and silent chamber, where they might seek the recovery of their health and reason; while the most simple works of nature, rejoiced in their full beauty and vigour. I could scarce forbear in ending this reflection, *crying out*, how ridiculous am I gentlemen, if I resemble you!

THE most weakned among them, however, still retained their pleasantry, when

when I saw the three women come
out, led by the most gallant, that is to
say, the most drunk.——I cannot pretend to do justice to this description,
but whoever will figure to themselves
three *Bacchanals* just coming out of
their fits of fury, will have the most
lively picture.——Their hair wildly di-
shevelled, their garments torn, their
flesh full of black and blue spots, and
scratched in many places; their eyes
heavy, their faces full of pimples.——
Odious to sight, and yet more so to
imagination.——I was going to take refuge in my coach, when the *Marquiss*
stopped me with a grave and solemn
air, as if about to unfold somewhat of
great importance. He had taken notice, that the womens clothes had suf-
fered a great deal by their readiness to
oblige the company, and took upon
him to represent to us, that if each of
them was obliged to buy a new gown
and head-dress, she would have little
remaining of her five *Lewis-d'rs*, and
we must not, *said he*, let merit go
naked out of our hands. We are eight
of us, *he continued,* let us add two

Lewis-

Lewis-d'rs a-piece to the fum agreed
upon. *Then turning to the women,* he
defired they would not be offended at
the injury done to their cloaths, which
had been occafioned only by the effect of
their charms, and to take on themfelves
the care of buying new robes. I willingly gave my two *Lewis-d'rs,* laughing within myfelf, at this comical un-
ravelling that miftery which had feemed couched in the beginning of the
Marquifs's harangue. As I was going
away, *Fanchon* approached to give me
her hand: Ah, madamoifelle, *faid I,*
all the waters of the *Danube* will never
wafh off what I fee. She did not feem
to comprehend the meaning of my
words, and I went into my coach.----
The *Chevalier* called out to me, that
he hoped to fee me again the firft fupper he made. Yes, *anfwered I,* if I
am not buried to-morrow. Go, go,
*rejoined the old Marquifs, with a hoarfe
voice,* we fhall have you again.

I heard him, without making any
reply, being refolved within myfelf, not
to

to enter a second time into these kind
of amusements; but I was too much
overcome with sleep, to be capable of
much reflection; I leaned back in my
coach, giving all my faculties up to
repose, and was scarce awake, when I
came home: my *valet de chambre*, put
me to bed like an infant, and though I
did not rise till six o'clock at night,
thought the time I had lain was very
short.

THE first thing that presented itself
to me, was a letter from my father,
which had been brought that morning
by the post. I stood indeed of something very interesting to dissipate those
ideas which were rising in my mind,
on the adventures of the preceding
night; but this proved much more so,
than I could have imagined. He wrote
to me all the circumstances of an inci-
dent that seemed so strange to me, that
after reading the letter, I could not forbear thinking I was still asleep.——I
examined it again and again, and the
more I did so, the more was my astonishment increased.——He acquainted
me,

me, that fince my departure, his friends
having preffed him to marry, he had
determined upon it with no difficulty,
as I was in poffeffion of five and twenty thoufand livres a year, and therefore
he hoped, independent on any thing
he had to bequeath, though had it been
otherwife, there was little likelihood,
that, at his age, his marriage would be
any prejudice to my expectations: in
fine, thefe confiderations, *he faid,* had
engaged him to offer his hand to madamoifelle *de St. V.* that lady having
but a fmall fortune, he had flattered
himfelf would have excufed his age, in
regard of the advantages he had propofed to her, and then *proceeded to tell
me,* that her father and mother having
agreed on every thing with him, he attended not the formalities of courtfhip,
but defired the celebration might be
fpeedy; on which articles were drawn
between them, a day appointed for the
marriage, and the friends invited.----
After this, *he went on with his narrative;* the night preceding the morning
of his intended nuptials, fhe threw herfelf at her father's feet, and with abundance

dance of tears, entreated his pardon,
for having concealed her situation. Said
it was fear, and respect, which had hitherto obliged her to be silent, but now
being so near plunging herself into the
worst of crimes, she was emboldned
by her remorse : confessed that she had
long loved me, and had thought herself not less beloved by me; that I had
indeed left her with cruelty enough,
but in the time of our mutual confidence, she had shewn me some complaisances, which would not permit her
to be the wife of my father.——That
having declared thus much, she produced a letter from me since my departure, which though cold enough, testified the change she accused me of, and
confirmed the truth of her complaints,
since, in it, I had desired her to forget
me, and confessed, that the thoughts
of war, and raising my fortune and
reputation, had made me renounce
love.——*My father added*, *that* having
torn the marriage articles, he was in
haste for nothing so much as to reproach me for incurring him the danger of falling into incest.——That this
ad-

adventure, which had been made no
fecret, had drawn many railleries, to
the prejudice of madamoifelle *de St. V.*
That he could impute my behaviour
only to a weaknefs which he was
grieved to find me capable of; but as
it had influenced me to abufe the confidence and inclinations of a maid of
condition, he did not think I ought on
any pretence, to abandon her.——And
that the profpects I had of fortune,
muft not be preferred to thofe of Honour.——He concluded with exhorting
me to remember, that he had never
given me other example, nor preached
other maxims to me, than thofe he at
prefent recommended.

In the agitation I was, after having
well confidered the purport of this letter, I began to call to mind all that
had paffed between madamoifelle *de
St. V. * * *,* and me, in the few vifits I had made her.——My heart and
my memory were equally witneffes for
me on this occafion; I found, that fo
far from making any attempt upon her
virtue, I never had entertained, even

in

in the illusions of sleep, the least thought
of that kind. What, *said I to myself*,
can then have been the occasion of her
attacking me with such fables? it is an
artifice inspired by love, or resentment?
or is it owing to a disgust she has conceived to my father, that she has had
recourse to an invention, which, though
unjust and strange, assured her of being
delivered from his importunities.——I
then run over as much as I could, the
particulars of my letter, in order to find
what arms I had furnished her with a-
gainst me. I recollected that I had made
use of some terms which being capable of
being understood two ways, that which
served her purpose was made choice of.
I was loth to dress my refusal of her
passion in expressions too plain, and I
now perceived my politeness was inter-
preted love, and yet I had imagined I
was as explicit as good breeding would
allow.——I found, however, by the manner in which my father treated this affair, that his good opinion of madamoiselle *de St. V.* * * *, would render
it extremely difficult to erace the false
ideas she had inspired him with. I resolved,

solved, however, to attempt it, and
began to anfwer his letter with invoking
Honour and Truth to be the director
of my pen, and then protefted, that I
never had any fort of engagements with
madamoifelle *de St. V. * * **, for which
fhe could reproach me, and humbly be-
feeched him, not to regard any equivo-
cal expreffions fhe might make ufe of to
that end, but demand of her to relate in
plain terms, on what fhe founded her
accufation. I begged him alfo to communicate this letter to her, and obferve
her countenance while reading it, as
well as the anfwers fhe fhould give to
him on the contents.

I enclofed alfo a feparate billet in
this letter, wherein I entreated him not
to condemn me without farther proofs
than the infinuations of a woman, for
whom I never had felt any emotions
beyond a bare refpect. But after I had
finifhed thefe difpatches, I fell into reflections which inflicted on me a good
deal of difquiet. A maid of birth and
reputation, was about to demean the
one, and lofe the other, on my account.

count. The blame muſt either fall on me, or on herſelf, and in the ſeverity with which I had been accuſtomed to judge of my own actions, I was afraid even to give my innocence its due, and this unhappy adventure to which indeed I owe moſt of the ſucceeding miſeries of my life, continued to engroſs my thoughts, when word was brought me, that the *Marquiſs* was come to viſit me ; he entered my chamber the ſame inſtant, and after having aſked me how I liked our libertine entertainment, invited me to accompany him that night to ſupper at the caſtle *de E.* * *, where he had already preſented me. I readily conſented to go with him, but told him, in regard to that party, which had engaged us the precedent night, and of which he had ſo much boaſted, I was determined never to paſs another in the ſame manner. I told him, thoſe extraordinary excitements to amorous inclinations, might ſuit well enough with his age, but not with mine.---That the behaviour of the women was a ſort of *Cantharides*, which my years had no neceſſity of.---I choſe to teſtify my de-
teſtation

teftation of thofe infamous orgies in this air of raillery, becaufe I would not be thought to fet up for a reformer, and knew that to converfe with any freedom in the World, it was moft prudent to fhut ones eyes to what we could not approve. I did not fail, however, to defire him, in the moft ferious terms, to make my excufes to the *Chevalier* and his friends, and to lay the blame of my abfence on the care I was obliged to take of my health, which, if he pleafed, he might tell them, I had fome reafon to apprehend.

While I was dreffing, the *Marquifs* took up a book to amufe himfelf, and I recollected, during this interval, not only the debaucheries I had been witnefs of, but alfo the licentious difcourfes of thofe people, which had no regard, either to the reputation of their friends, nor the refpect due to religion.---What virtue, what good quality, either civil or military, *faid I to my felf*, can there be expected, where there is fo total a forgetfulnefs of the firft principles of human fociety? I would

would not truſt my purſe, nor ſleep in
the ſame bed with one, who thought
himſelf bound by no moral obligations:
when probity has no foundation in the
heart; the fear of infamy is inſufficient
to defend us from being guilty of a baſe
action, becauſe cunning may enable us
to conceal it; neither can even that happy diſpoſition ſome people receive from
nature be depended upon, becauſe ſick-
neſs, paſſion, or misfortune may ſour
the ſweeteſt temper.---How then can a-
ny one pretend to affirm, that there may
be a truly honeſt man without religion,
or regard for his neighbour? what can
be the object of probity, if it is not god
or mankind?

THE *Marquiſs* who had only taken
up a book before my people, had not leſs
reflected on the diſlike I teſtified for my
laſt night's entertainment; and aſſoon
as we were alone, told me that I was too
much prejudiced againſt pleaſure.--That
indeed it had been carried to ſomewhat
of an exceſs the night before, but it was
not always ſo tumultuous.--That inſtead
of common women, they often had
E   thoſe

thofe that belonged to the *Opera,* and
fometimes even the wives of perfons
of condition, who were really honeft women, yet made no fcruple of partaking the
gaieties of the *Chevalier's* little pleafure
houfe.---He added, that I fhould chufe
which of thefe two forts fhould be invited to the next fupper, for as he was
mine, and my father's friend, he would
not wifh me to break off abruptly, with
perfons of quality, who fhewed a great
defire of cultivating a friendfhip with
me. This difcourfe appeared fo juft,
that I could not refufe affenting to it :
give me then the honeft women, *faid I,*
for befides the preference, my inclination gives them, I am curious too fee the
contrafte. · I confeffed to him, that I
found fo much wit and good humour
among the men of this affembly, that
I did not doubt but to be very happy
with them, at thofe times when they
confined their pleafures to innocent gallantry.

I went with him to the caftle *D'E**,*
where I paft an evening very little to
my fatisfaction : the company was chiefly

ly compofed of old lords and minifters of
ftate, with fome others, whom intereft,
rather than inclination brought to pay their
compliments to Monfieur *D'E***. Freedom and familiarity, the life of fociety,
feemed banifhed hence: they fmiled
without joy; they eat without relifh;
they difcourfed upon only fuch maxims
as were eftablifhed, and which none
would prefume to contradict: the wines
were very indifferent, in order as I fuppofe to preferve fobriety: no parties of
pleafure were propofed; and every one
departed with the fame ferious air with
which he had entered.

THE averfion I had conceived for
debauchery, did not make me forget the
promife I made to *Fanchon:* I was fe-
rioufly refolved to take her out of that
miferable fituation, and put her into
fome honeft way of getting her bread.--
The education fhe appeared to have,
made me imagine this would be no difficulty. Accordingly, I went in my
chair where fhe had directed, and found
her at home alone, and without paint.
I looked on this as a good fign, and far

from

from mortifying her with any mention
of what had paſt, I only aſked to what
kind of buſineſs her talent was moſt inclined; to which ſhe anſwered, that
ſhe believed, ſhe might make a living
by working with her needle, if ſhe
could get employment; and then told
me, that ſhe knew a *Milliner*, who
could be of great ſervice to her on this
occaſion; but that being a woman of
ſtrict virtue, ſhe had not courage to appear before her, after having behaved in
the manner I was not inſenſible of, and
which the other had doubtleſs been informed of. She mentioned this *Milli-*
ner in ſuch a manner, that I had not the
leaſt ſuſpicion of the deception was going to be put upon me; and I immediately told *Fanchon*, I would go myſelf
to the woman, and intereſt myſelf in
her behalf; on which ſhe gave me directions, and acknowledgments for my
goodneſs, too tedious to repeat.

In fine, I went, and found a woman
of a very grave and compoſed aſpect: I
no ſooner named *Fanchon*, and the buſineſs on which I came; then ſhe expreſſed

pressed the utmost concern for the fate
of that unfortunate girl, whose parents
she said were not unknown to her.—She
would have run on into a long detail, but
I interrupted the narrative, by telling
her, that what was done could not be
recalled, but might in some measure be
retrieved ; that I had no other design,
than to take *Fanchon* out of this wretched course of life, and related the means
by which I proposed it, entreating her
at the same time to second my charitable endeavours. She made some difficulty at first, at having any concern
with a girl who had so far forfeited her
reputation : but at length consented to
what I desired on two conditions ; the
first was, that she might be permitted to
acquaint her father and mother with
what I had done for her ; to the end
their knowledge of every thing might
render her conversion more constant ;
the other was, that I would add to my
benevolence, a small sum of money to
buy the furniture of a room for her, by
which, *said this hypocrite*, she will a-
void those occasions of falling into company, which is too often the case with

young

young women like her, by living in ready furnished lodgings.   To these terms
I readily yielded, and left the choice of
a convenient lodging for her, to herself,
whom I also desired to buy a bed, and o-
ther necessaries, the expence of all which
I would disburse on her bringing me the
bill.

Extremely pleased with the success of my negotiation, I never once
enquired into the character of the woman I had been treating with, which is
the only fault I can charge myself with,
in an adventure which indeed does little honour to my prudence ; but as it
was not strange, that a man of my sincerity, and who then was almost a
stranger in *Paris*, should be imposed
upon by such a shew of honesty and
virtue ; I write it for the instruction of
those who are of the same way of thinking with myself, and may have as little
experience as I had at that time.

Having confessed I was the dupe
of two vile creatures, I shall now shew
the gradual steps they took to prosecute
their

their deception on me.----*Fanchon* appeared transported with joy, when I told her my succeſs with madam *Birat*, for ſo the *Milliner* was called: I would not ſtay to hear the thouſand bleſſings ſhe was preparing to pour upon me: but other affairs taking me up for two days, I heard nothing of them ; but on the third, *Birat* came to me, and brought a bill of the goods ſhe had bought for the dear girl, as ſhe now kindly termed her. I looked it over, and found it amounted to fifteen hundred franks, but did not think the ſum too great to recover a young beautiful creature into the paths of honeſty and virtue ; and on the *Milliner*'s telling me, that *Fanchon* could not earn more than twenty ſols a day, it would be inſufficient to ſupport her, having been accuſtomed to eat well : I agreed to make her ſome allowance, in order to prevent her wanting any thing, that was neceſſary to prevent her relapſing through neceſſity into her former courſes ; and that this bounty ſhould be paid weekly, into the hands of *Birat*, who was to have the management of all.----Thus did both join to impoſe upon me ; but the ſequel will ſhew, that *Fanchon* was

herſelf

herself no lefs deceived by this wicked
confident.   I was alfo afterward informed, that it was through her infti-
gations, that fhe had become thus a-
bandoned ; that fhe brought her into
company, and made a confiderable advantage of her youth and beauty. She
had, however, ftill a farther defign upon me, but my good fortune difcovered
it, when juft on the point of being ex-
ecuted.   Not fufpecting I would ever
vifit *Fanchon*, as it was to her I paid
the penfion I allowed ; when ever fhe
came to receive it, fhe entertained me
with applaufes of my generofity, and
the difcretion of her penitent ; who
fhe faid was fo fearful of putting me to
any frefh expences, that fhe even denied
herfelf many things which fhe wanted ;
on which I told her, that rather than
fuffer her to do fo, I would make fome
addition to my allowance: but this fhe refufed to accept, which very much confirmed me in the belief of her fincerity.

THREE weeks having paffed on in
this manner, fhe came one day, and
with a well counterfeited air of gladnefs
                                        and

and simplicity; told me that heaven had given such a blessing to my charity, and presented the means of easing me of that burthen, my excess of generosity had laid upon me, and of rewarding *Fanchon* for her return to virtue.—One of the clerks of the farmers general, *added she*, has seen her by chance, and is so much in love with her, that he offers to marry her. On which I testifying the pleasure I took in hearing of her good fortune, gave her an opportunity of renewing the discourse in these terms. If the man, *said she*, was perfectly easy in his circumstances, we would not conceal from him the poverty of *Fanchon:* but alass he has met with difficulties, which I easily see will not permit him to marry, without some small portion with his wife; we were therefore, obliged to take the advantage of his ignorance of her affairs, and he does not doubt but that he shall have enough, at least to ease some incumbrances he has upon him, after which they may have a very comfortable life together. She concluded with asking me if I would put the finish-

ing

ing ftroke to the good work I had begun, in contributing fomething towards
removing this only bar, which was between *Fanchon* and a ftate of fettled
happinefs.   Without doubt I will, *replied I*, what do you think will fuffice?
I believe, *faid fhe*, not lefs than a thoufand crowns.   If this wretch had demanded two thoufand, I fhould have
given them, on an occafion which I
thought fo laudable;   but I affured her
the fum fhe mentioned fhould be paid
on the day of marriage, and that I
would alfo add fome jewels, which
might ferve to remind *Fanchon*, both of
my friendfhip, and the fource of it.
Madame *Birat* then fixed the day for
the wedding, and I defired her to take
care it fhould be folemnized with decency.

Never had I been fenfible of a
more perfect fatisfaction than at that
time; the virtue and the happinefs of
an amiable perfon, feemed entirely the
work of my hands; and I returned
thanks to heaven, for making me the
inftrument of this good action, and
                                    wanted

wanted methought to communicate the
tranſport, which was indeed too great
for me to contain.   As I had never ſeen
Fanchon ſince *Birat* had taken charge
of her, I could not reſiſt the deſire of
congratulating her, on ſo unexpected an
effect of her charms.   I went therefore
to her lodging the morning preceding
that which was appointed for her nuptials ; and as I thought there was no neceſſity for ceremony, ſent no word of
my approach.   I found her at home ;
but perceived a ſtrange confuſion in her
looks at ſeeing me enter ; which however, I did not at that time endeavour to
account for.   I embraced her tenderly,
which was the firſt time I had ever
given her that token of my friendſhip
and eſteem.   Heaven is my witneſs, *ſaid
I*, that I rejoice, as much in your happineſs as you, yourſelf can do.----Ah !
continued I, how adorable is beauty,
when accompanied with honour and
virtue! the man to whom you are going
to give your hand will be happy.----
To-morrow, *added I*, is it not to-morrow your marriage is to be ſolemnized ?
Fanchon ſurprized beyond meaſure at
E 6   my

my words; *cried out*, me married!
Monseigneur? pardon me if I do not
comprehend this pleasantry. O! *answered I*, Madame *Briat* has told me
all, and I hope you are satisfied with the
proofs I have promised of my approbation? her amazement seeming to re-
double; are you not *said I*, to be married to-morrow to a *Clerk* of the
Farmer's-*general?* Good heaven! *said
she lifting up her eyes*, I know no such
man; nor is there any one has made me
such an offer. I was now much more a-
mazed than she had been; but easily perceiving I had been imposed upon; I
started from my chair in the first emotions of my rage; walked two or three
times about the room, scarce knowing
where I was; called for my footmen
without having any commands to give
them; but they no sooner appeared,
than I grew somewhat more calm, and I
reflected that if *Fanchon* had joined in this
piece of treachery, she would not have
denied the pretended marriage, nor have
been surprized at the mention I made of
it.

HER

HER aftonifhment had rendered her immoveable in the chair fhe was feated in; I now took one and drew near her, repeated all the circumftances Madame *Birat* had related to me, and omitted not the thoufand crowns I had promifed. While I was fpeaking, I perceived an indignation not inferior to my own, rife in her eyes and cheeks: and when I had given over, Madame *Birat* is the moft wicked woman in the world, *faid fhe*, fhe has deceived both you and me; nor is this the firft bafe action fhe has been guilty of to both.—The furniture you fee here coft but five hundred franks, and fhe made you pay fifteen hundred. The reft fhe put in her own pocket to pay herfelf, as fhe faid, for the trouble fhe had taken; and this made me not doubt but fhe would ftill defraud me, which indeed fhe did; and I had wrote to acquaint you, that fhe never paid me any more than one half of the penfion you allowed me, if I had not been reftrained by the fears of her doing me fome worfe prejudice.

As I found nothing in this recital, to condemn *Fanchon*, I was going to lament the unhappiness of her situation; which I imagined, she had been involved in, only by having too good an opinion of *Birat*; when, all on a sudden, I felt a curiosity of examining more nearly those goods, for which I paid so dear. How could I be so blinded *cried I*, rising from my chair, in order to go into the next room, where *Fanchon* had her bed. — She suspected my design, and ran between me and the door, endeavouring to make me turn back; by saying, she had more to tell me of that base woman: but though I suspected no artifice in her behaviour, I pursued my thought, and pushed open the door. Going in, I found a man dressing himself, who, turning towards me, asked in a resolute voice, if I wanted any thing with him? no, *answered I carelesly*, I am only sorry to have disturbed you; for after passing the night with *Madamoiselle*, you might probably not have chose to rise so early. In the condition you

have

have surprized me, *replied he smiling*, it would be ridiculous, to make a secret of my business here. — But I should be extremely sorry, *added he, in the most complaisant tone*, to have interfered with your interests. Not at all I assure you, *said I*, she can tell you, I came on a quite different affair. After this discovery, my curiosity was entirely extinguished; and I flung out of the room, without saying one word to *Fanchon*.

It would have been easy for me, to have punished two wretches, who had so unworthily abused my bounty, and good nature; but I looked upon them, as beneath my revenge; and thought also, that revenge was beneath me. I disdained either to trouble the one, for her frauds; or to confound the other, by way of reproaches, for her indiscretion.— The *Marquiss*, to whom I related this adventure, mortified my credulity, by telling me, that he not only knew *Birat*, was a merchant of pleasures, as well as modes; but likewise, that it was she, who had brought

Fanchon

Fanchon, and her two companions, to that debauch, where I had firſt ſeen her.   He added, that *Fanchon*, had purſued the ſame irregular courſe, ſhe had been accuſtomed to; while I imagined her buſily employed, in a laudable occupation.   I know, *ſaid he*, by frequent experiences, that women of this ſort are incapable of being reclaimed: in that weak ſex, the leaſt taſte of debauchery is a poiſon, which in an inſtant corrupts both nature and education.----I compare this infection of the mind, to that ſhameful diſeaſe of the body, which proceeds from the ſame ſourſe: if you aſk a phyſician, he will tell you, that dreadful chaſtiſement of a brutal appetite, communicates itſelf immediately through the whole maſs of blood, as the juice of a lemon corrupts a baſon of milk.   A woman therefore in her firſt debauch, has all the good qualities of her ſoul tainted and perverted, nothing of innocence remains, but in her form; which often deceives a worthy man unſkilled in the artifices of vice.

I

I would not teſtify the gratitude I owed to heaven, for enduing me with ſuch principles, as alone, have power to join happineſs with proſperity; and ſoften the pangs of the moſt ſevere calamity; till I had given my readers an occaſion to ſee I had ſome right, to attribute them to my character; which I ſhall now take the liberty, to delineate more fully. I was formed for the pleaſures of life, by my birth; my education, my natural qualities, and above all, by my inclinations, and reliſh of them; but it was for rational pleaſures, that I was formed; and theſe propenſities, which ſeemed moſt eſtimable in my own eyes, were thoſe which I found leaſt of, in the ſocieties I had been among: I perceived neverthelefs, that thoſe who were ſtrangers to them themſelves, did not diſlike me, for putting them in practice. The averſion I had for ſcandal, and the readineſs with which I eſpouſed the cauſe of an abſent perſon, I found was not diſagreeable to moſt people, as I took care to treat the detractor with politeneſs,
and

and never carried my zeal into ill-manners. The honour of heaven above all things I never could ſuffer to be traduced, and always maintained that in all events, an entire reſignation to the will of the firſt being, and the author of all benefits, was the indiſpenſible duty of mortals; and in this I alſo found, that even thoſe who by ſome unhappy conſiderations were hindered from joining with me, were not diſpleaſed with my endeavouring to perſuade them to it. But there was one difficulty I met with, which ſometimes made me very uneaſy. It was not meer ignorance; for I very well knew every one had not an equal ſhare of underſtanding; nor was it even that preſumption and tenaciouſneſs of opinion, with which ſome men think to over bear their auditors; for I was ſenſible that vanity and ſelf-love in a more or leſs degree, are natural to all that breath; but it was the defect of juſtice in their arguments, and their reaſoning on falſe principles that gave me pain. What could I underſtand of a diſcourſe, which was not only oppoſite to truth, but conſiſted of points even
op-

opposite to each other ! an insult upon
my honour, could scarcely have been
more offensive to me ; but my politeness forbid me to take notice of it, and
all the remedy I had, was to make no
reply : the speaker took my silence as a
mark of my approbation, and those who
knew better, regarded it as the reserve
of a man, whose modesty would not
permit him to shew his own good sense
at the expence of others. I was less cau-
tious concerning the little frauds and de-
ceptions, which I saw frequently put in
practice, by those who in other respects
passed for honest men ; but which extremely shocked the uprightness and generosity of my nature : those of play,
for example ; but though I could not
restrain myself from taking notice, I
never exposed my observations to any
other, than the person guilty of them.
Being one day where they were play-
ing at *Quadrille*, I perceived an *Abbé*
whom I happened to sit near, had the
cunning whenever he shuffled the cards,
to drop *Spadille* and *Basto* on his knees
under the table, dealing two cards short
of his number to himself, which he afterwards

terwards fupplied with thefe two aces.
I faw him do this fo often, and fweep
fo much money by the artifice, that I
could not reftrain myfelf from whifper-
ing to him : Monfieur *L' Abbé*, if this
practice continues, I fhall be obliged to
expofe you.

ANOTHER time at a *Phara* table,
I faw a man of condition, mark *Sept*
and *le Va*, for the *Paroli*. This ftrata-
gem had frequently fucceeded. Ah!
Monfieur, *faid I to him foftly*, will the
profit compenfate for the fhame if difcovered? befides, the difdain I had for
all injuftice of this kind, I never difpu-
ted any doubtful point in whatever game
I engaged in ; chufing rather to be ac-
counted ignorant of the rules, than give
any occafion for quarrel.

IT is certain that people in general,
have an idea of thofe virtues which they
leaft exercife.---I have often obferved,
that the moft abandoned, affect an efteem for thofe qualities, which are the
oppofites of their own vices, whether it
be that they think to difguife themfelves
by

by this diffimulation; or that they cannot help paying fome reverence to virtue, I will not pretend to determine; but
I found my company follicited with ear-
neftnefs, by thofe very perfons whom I
expected would have fhunned me on account of my principles: the old *Marquifs*, though fometimes a little angry
with me, for the diflike I expreffed of
thofe pleafures he had fo high a relifh
of, could not keep himfelf from praife-
ing the conduct I preferved. He fpoke
of the affair relating to *Fanchon* where
ever he came, and though there were
fome who pretended to fay, that if I
was mafter of that good fenfe the world
allowed me, I could not have been
fuch a dupe; yet the greateft number
both of men and women highly applauded that action.

THESE reflections, have carried me
from the Supper, to which I was engaged; but I fhall now return, I went
in the morning, to pay my compliment
to the *Chevalier*, as the director, and
head of the pleafures, we were to enjoy:
he told me the names of thofe ladies,
who were to honour us with their company:

pany: there were four of them, all *said he*, are women of condition, and set so high a value on their reputation, that in spite of the good opinion, they have of me, they would not risque it, by coming to my little recess, if not defended from censure by their number. One, *continued he*, is the wife of a *Commodore*, who lives in little restraint at *Paris*; while her husband is cruising on the coasts of *Africk*, she is at all balls, feasts, and public assemblies; but her virtue, is defended by her vanity. She has got it into her head, that gallantry is destructive of beauty, especially the complexion; and hers, being extremely find, she prefers the preservation of her charms, and the certain admiration paid to them, to those sweets, which are not always to he found in love.

BUT, *added he*, though she has so great an indifference for the men, they pretend to say, she has not the same, for the wine of *Champaigne*, which is not less an enemy to the complexion; and some, who are more malicious than I, will tell you, she is proof on both sides.

ANOTHER

ANOTHER of our ladies, *continued he*, is the *Counteſs de Z * * **, ſhe is a brown beauty, witty, but ſatirical ; and devoted to gaming. I had heard this name before, and the better remembered it, by her love of play : on my aſking the *Chevalier*, if I had not ſeen her with madam, the lady of the *Intendant of * * **; I believe you have, *ſaid he*, for ſhe is one of her friends. I think her very amiable, *rejoined I*, and am very ſorry her paſſion for play, lays her under the neceſſity of being obliged to a *Financier*, whom they deſcribe to me, as a man no way qualified to gratify the inclinations of a fine lady. O ! *replied the Chevalier*, ſhe has no inclinations but for gaming: this *Financier* you mention is her *Dupe*, but not her *Lover* :— he loves play as much as ſhe, and imagines he underſtands it, though he always loſes. We had a party two days ago at *Picquet*, he played againſt the *Counteſs* and myſelf : twelve livres the point, we had the better of him conſiderably, as indeed we never fail of doing, and I believe we have won of him

this

this winter, about a hundred thoufand livres. — Whether it be, that having loft fo much, he is eager to regain it, or, that the vanity, as you fay, of being thought well with the *Countefs*, I know not; but he is continually propofing fome new engagement of this kind. — I give you my word, however, *purfued he*, that there is nothing like an amour between them. I thought it needlefs, to tell the *Chevalier*, what my fentiments were, on the recital he gave me; which was fo plain a proof, of the little inclination our *Intendant*'s lady had, to put the beft conftruction on any thing.

OUR third lady, *refumed he*, is indeed a very beautiful woman, whom I fhould think myfelf happy to pleafe, but though I have continued to tell her fo, for two years, my fuit is not at all advanced: but I afcribe not her cruelty, to any paffionate attachment to her hufband; for he is wholly taken up with a Girl, that fings at the *Opera*, and gives himfelf not the leaft pain, about the conduct of his wife: this behaviour of his

his, would have given me some suspicion of her, if I had not made it my
business to observe all her actions with
the utmost care ; and though she is far
from having an aversion to the other
pleasures, I find there is a certain cold-
ness in her constitution, which defends
her from the assaults of love.

To conclude, *continued he*, you will
sup to night with a fourth beauty, who
has not been always so averse to mankind as at present.---She had a favourite
lover, whose death has left a settled melancholly on her spirits, yet is she nevertheless extremely charming.

I expected at the beginning of this
discourse, to have found pictures of the
same nature with those, I had received
from madame the *Intendant*'s lady ; but
the *Chevalier* ceased|without|mingling any
gall among his colours.-I have all my life
observed, that the women are mostly fond
of detraction and calumny, even against
those to whom they bear no ill-will, as
if scandal were inherent to their nature ;
whereas the men are rarely guilty of it,

F   un-

unlefs heated with wine, excited by example, or provoked by ill ufage. I accompanied the *Chevalier* to the *Opera*,
and then to his recefs of pleafure.--The
ladies did not come in fome time after:
the moon which fpread a beautiful light
through all the horrizon, made us not
regret the abfence of the fun in the walk
we took in the garden, where we paft
our time till fupper: we were fix men,
for the ladies had exacted that there
fhould be an inequality of number of
the two fexes, to avoid an air of parti-
cularity in this meeting. Their eyes
were immediately caft upon the ftatues
before mentioned.---Ay fie, *cried the
melancholy beauty*, one would think on-
felf among the *Indians*; I cannot conceive how any one can have a tafte for
thefe indecent objects.---The *Chevalier*
threw the fault on the *Sculpture*, as the
Sculpture doubtlefs would on him who
employed him. It looks methinks, *faid
the commodore's wife*, as if you intended
to bring us into a fnare, but there can
be no danger in marble, when we have
nothing elfe to apprehend. You are
right madame, interrupted the countefs,
and

and I dare say they never thought of us
when these filthy images were set up,
and had them only to gratify their own
imaginations.---However, *said the lady
who had the preference in the Chevalier's
esteem*, a gallant man ought not to suffer such spectacles to be exhibited before women. What a contrast did I
find between the present discourse, and
the shouts of laughter, and gross repartees which these statues had occasioned at our first supper. We continued to walk, and the conversation was
neither very lively, nor very stupid;
neither fine, nor without wit, but wholly
free from all disorder and indecorum: e-
very one spoke what presented itself to his
thoughts.---One recounted the news of
the day; another took occasion to bring
to mind some history of a more ancient
date. The ladies sung, and the men
gave their opinions, as to the airs and
the words; in fine, nothing interesting
employed the tongues, or I believe the
minds of any of the company, till the
major Domo appeared with his napkin
under his arm, to let us know the table
was served; and while we passed from

the

the garden to the hall, the time was taken up with praifing the good grace and addrefs of this domeftic.

WE found the table furnifhed in a manner becoming the politenefs and fortune of the *Chevalier* : and the room being prodigioufly light by a great number of wax candles, I had the opportunity of obferving more clearly the charms of thefe ladies. But though they were all perfectly agreeable, I found them infinitely inferior to *Fanchon* in the beauty of the face; and I could not forbear complaining of nature, for being for the moft part lefs liberal to women of quality, than to thofe without birth, and without honour. But when I confidered that rank and degree, were only forms eftablifhed by men, to which nature was not fubjected; I allowed the juftice of her difpenfations in this point: thofe who could have no title to refpect but by their beauty, muft have been miferable without it, whereas thofe endued with other qualifications, ftand in no need of it.

BUT

BUT to return to our entertainment: the plates were filled with all the season produced of elegant and rare : the wines were excellent, and we all seemed to eat with a good appetite, yet notwithstanding there appeared an air of reserve in the whole company, which in my opinion was constrained : all the women mingled water with their wine, scarce could be persuaded to touch *Champaign :* they tasted the ragooes and fricasses, but like a bird that seems afraid of soiling its feathers : I excused these little affectaions, on account of an over delicacy of stomach ; but was surprized to find them testify so little relish for pleasantry, in a place to which they came merely to indulge, with all innocent liberties, the gaiety of the heart. On the contrary, all was dull and formal : during the first course the wife of the *Commodore* entertained us with a discourse, which in its beginning I found would be heavy enough. After admiring the elegance and propriety of the house, she spoke of the uses to which those recesses are generally ordained, and

then

then told us, she believed the pleasures we found here, were not always
restrained within the same bounds as at
present. On this all the ladies began
to rally the inclinations of mankind,
and the complaisance with which
the lower part of women were sometimes treated. We defended ourselves as
well as we could, and in being asked
a thousand questions, which it was
not proper should be answered with
sincerity, were obliged to equivocate,
deny many things, and disguise all.
This discussion was carried on with
an air of prudery in the discourse of
the women ; and of constraint in that
of the men, and after having wasted a
long time in this manner, the four ladies thought themselves obliged to keep
up to the utmost punctilio's of behaviour, in order to shew us the difference between them, and those with
which they had reproached us. It
was impossible to get them out of this
humour, and the *Marquiss*, who had
said some spirituous things for that end,
was desired to hold his tongue, and
exhorted, with an ironical smile, to
re-

referve thofe military witicifms for o-
ther company. Thus with the beft
chear in the world, and every thing
neceffary to promote a fprightly converfation, four women, who were really very amiable, and fix men, who
wanted not wit, nor good humour, paft
an evening with all the folemnity of a
funeral.

We did not fit very long at table,
but our rifing was only a prolongation
of dulnefs: when once that peft of fociety, called dulnefs, has crept into
the mind, adieu gaiety, gallantry, attention to circumftances, and relifh for
the beft things. They talked of retiring the moment fupper was over,
but the coaches were not ordered till
two hours after, fo we all adjourned to
the drawing-room, where, indeed,
each appeared fomewhat more at
eafe.

The ladies placed themfelves on the
couch and carpet, and none of the men
approached near them in that pofture,
nor even feemed to have a defire of

doing

doing fo : on which I could not keep
myfelf from recollecting that fcene of
libertinifm which had been practifed
in the fame place fome days before.   I
was ftruck to fee four women of virtue, take up thofe feats, which had
been the theatre of the moft profligate
diffolution.   What difference did I
now find in the vivacity of my companions ? Scarce could I comprehend
how it came to pafs that the converfation of the debauched part of the fex,
fhould make them lofe their tafte for
that of women of honour and merit,
yet I found it was effectually fo, and
that they regretted the abfence of *Fan-*
chon, *Catin*, and *Licetta*.

NEVERTHELESS the old *Marquifs*,
who was looked upon among them
as the promoter of mirth, thought it
incumbent upon him to rouze us, if
poffible out of this lethargic ftate : in
order to which, he attempted to engage the ladies on fome topics of gallantry, but confined himfelf to the bounds
he perceived they were determined to
preferve ; he told them they were not
                                                    fuffi-

sufficiently armed against the power of
sleep, but that he could put them in
the head of a most excellent preser-
vative, which was for every one in her
turn to relate the history of some interesting part of her own life; for, *said
he*, recitals of this nature have an infinitely better grace when coming from
your sex, and therefore I must entreat,
not only for our sakes, but your own,
that you will favour us with this a-
musement. With all my heart, *replied the countess*, I will begin as an
example to the others.

I lived till sixteen years, *said she*,
without being acquainted with any man
besides my father, my brothers, and
my cousin-germans; for I came but at
that age from a convent, where no
others were permitted to approach me.
One day, as I was walking alone in
the garden belonging to our seat in the
country, I perceived the most beautiful bird I had ever seen, perched upon
the wall, without seeming afraid of
me. I advanced nearer that I might
observe it better; on which it flew

softly

softly away, but being out of sight, immediately I imagined it could not be far from the other side of the wall, and opened a little door which gave into the fields, where I indeed saw the pretty animal hopping about upon the grafs, and ran full of the hopes of catching it, which I did with a great deal of eafe, and was highly delighted with the prize I had got. As I was juft returning to the garden, a young man, of an agreeable afpect, ftarted from behind a thicket, where he had concealed himfelf, and told me, in a tone full of complaifance, that having loft his bird, he was tranfported to fee it in my hands. I then offered to return it to him, though indeed with a good deal of regret, but was furprized to hear him fay; no, madam, let him live in thofe divine hands, and would to heaven I had the fame fate for my whole life. My aftonifhment did not hinder me from viewing him with attention. His perfon and addrefs feemed charming to me ; I permitted him the opportunity that inftant of declaring his paffion. He told me, that impatient

patient to assure me of it, he had watched my hours of walking, and that love had inspired him with this innocent artifice : in fine, I took his bird, and he took me in return ; that is to say, having won me to receive his courtship, he became my husband with the consent of my father.

THE *Countess* added to this little narrative many graces, which I have not been able to retain ; but remember, that she had no sooner finished, than the wife of the *Commodore* cry'd, now I will recount to you one of my adventures.

THE world knows, *said she,* that without condemning others, I make profession of a strict fidelity to my husband, who has been so two years this day. He has been absent from me five or six months together, and I believe every one will acknowledge, that time must appear very tedious to a woman who loves. I have been surrounded with temptations, but I am established in principles which leaves me nothing

to

to fear on thofe occafions. Yet one night, as I was in a found fleep, a dream prefented itfelf to me, little to the honour of my husband: it was this. The moft dangerous of all my lovers, after having done a thoufand fervices to merit my efteem, feemed to me in fleep to have gained more upon me, than my waking hours ever beftowed on him; I thought I loved him, and that the careffes he gave me were fo tranfporting, that endeavouring to repulfe him, I found it the fevereft facrifice I could make to my duty. However, the pleafure ftole more and more upon my heart; my whole frame was in agitation; I trembled leaft I fhould not be able to refift the united force of his preffures and my own inclinations: in fine, at laft imagining all my refolution entirely overcome, I awaked in the fright, and thinking I was lock'd in the embraces of fome one, was fo in effect, and found myfelf in the arms of my husband.

As this recital gave occafion to many pleafantries, the lady haftily added, that

Candida

Voltaire

DQ
2682
C3
25 X
1966

PQ
2081
25
B4

le Montesquieu
lettre
persannes

PQ
281
25
T5

La abbe prevost

PQ
2021
MF75
(Fransios d'Exiles

life of Antoine
prevost

Fr trans.

Card

Library of Congress Classification

Dewey Decimal Classification

that in the innocence of her heart, and the joy ſhe had at ſeeing the *Commodore*, who ſhe knew not was returned till ſhe found him in bed, ſhe made no ſcruple of telling him her dream, and that he was very much diverted with it.   The *Marquiſs*, who had taken an averſion to this woman, whiſpered in my ear, what do we learn by this adventure, but that the husband is a fool, and the wife little better ? To which I replied, that in a woman truly virtuous, I found nothing impoſſible in what ſhe ſaid.

THE melancholy lady could not be diſpenſed with from giving us alſo her little hiſtory.   A deep ſigh, which was the prelude of her diſcourſe, would have made me know the ſituation of her heart, if the *Chevalier* had not before informed me of it.   Alas ! *ſaid ſhe*, you demand of me ſomewhat to amuſe you ! Where ſhall I find ſubject for it ? I have long ſince done with mirth, and find nothing in my memory but matters of affliction : nevertheleſs I ſhall comply with your requeſts. I.
had,

had, *continued she, renewing her sighs,*
about six months ago, a tame turtle
dove, which I loved with the extremest
tenderness: the dear animal was not insensible of my kindness: he was never
easy but when with me: the least absence from me gave him a visible affliction. I imagined I discovered in him
all the qualities that are attributed to his
species, and am much deceived, if he
had not for me all that one *turtle-dove*
can feel for another. What, shall I
tell you there is nothing to divert you
in this narrative but its singularity?
One day, when I was caressing my precious *turtle*, a frightful beast, the horror of nature, a beast to which I cannot give a name, but am surprized I
could see so near me without dying,
came in, and snatched my lovely bird
from my arms, regardless of my cries
or tears: never since have I beheld
my poor *turtle*, but I shall always love
him.

THIS disconsolate lady did not imagine we were so well acquainted with
the motive of her grief: it is the error
of

of many women at *Paris*, to flatter
themselves with a belief their intrigues
are not discovered, and the public is frequently more apt to give credit to false
appearances, than to penetrate into those
which are real. But as we knew the
truth, we easily comprehended that she
found an ease in venting her sentiments,
by giving us the history of her loss,
which she fancied was so well disguised
under this allegory. The *turtle dove*
was her lover, and the cruel beast which
one could not see without dying was
death itself. There was none in the
company, but what was touched with
her sorrows, especially when they saw
some tears fall from her eyes, as she left
off speaking.

THE beautiful object of the *Chevalier*'s admiration was reserved for the last,
in spite of the cruelty he complained
of, I perceived she maintained a kind of
empire over him; which convincing
her how much she was beloved, made
her perhaps without design, naturally
do the honours of the house, and behave in a manner as the mistress of it.
She wanted little courtship to oblige us
in

in the manner the other ladies had done,
and readily prefented us with the following ftory.

ONE is fometimes engaged, *faid fhe*,
without any intention to be fo. Laft
fummer having dined at the houfe of a
neighbour of mine in the country, I
returned home towards evening with
my woman, whom I had made accompany me in this vifit. Two gentlemen
who happened to dine at the fame place,
were fo gallant to efcorte my chariot on
horfeback. The fame politenefs made
them alight at my door, in order to
hand me out: the weather being very
warm, my woman who is pretty fat,
having been wiping her face all the way
we came with a white handkerchief,
happened to let it fall at the bottom of
the chariot; one of the gentlemen in
giving me his hand perceived it, and
believing it mine, catched it up with a
kind of tranfport. I underftood fo little the aim of this country gallantry,
that I afked him what made him ftoop
for fuch a trifle; on which he put it into his pocket, humbly befeeching me
ta

to grant him that satisfaction : O ! willingly, *answered I*, and immediately quitted him and went into my house. I never thought of speaking of this affair to my woman, but two days after she brought me a letter without any superscription, which I opening hastily, found it was from the same gentleman, containing a thousand acknowledgements for the favour I had bestowed on him, and as many assurances that he had done nothing since he saw me, but kiss that divine handkerchief. I found the mistake so pleasant, that I resolved to add to it ; and calling my woman, told her the letter was to herself. She finding so many passionate declarations, of which she doubted not but she was the object as not having heard what passed between the gentleman and I on the score of the handkerchief, formed a high idea of having her fortune made by so heroic a passion. The expectation she was in, was extremely diverting to me : eight days, however, passed without our hearing any thing farther, but he then came to visit me : I had a great deal of company at that time, and
we

we were at play, but I received him
civilly, and he found an opportunity
when my hand was out, to speak to
me without witnesses : nothing certainly ever came up to the extravagancies
he entertained me with.----His violent
passion.--His gratitude for my conde-
scension. His adoration of the divine
handkerchief; the ardour with which
he kissed it night and day.---In fine, not
able to keep myself from laughing, I
resolved to put an end to the scene : you
take me for another, *said I*, and have
less obligation to me than you think ;
but I see the cause of your mistake. I
then called my woman, and asked her
if she had not dropt a handkerchief,
she had made a great deal of use of the
day we dined at Monsieur *de S* * * ?
she answered with some confusion that
she had.   Well then, *said I*, here is
the gentleman that has found it.

THERE was nothing in this story
very enchanting, to any, besides the
Chevalier ; who, as soon as she had
done, has she not a grace peculiar to
herself, *cried he to me*, in the relation
she

she has given us? She had indeed, in the tone of her voice; but, as for the subject and turn of expression, I thought the *Countess*, excelled both her, and the other two ladies. Every one, has not the talent of telling a story agreeably; and those, who have it not by nature, cannot acquire it, without infinite difficulty. Nothing, notwithstanding is more pleasing, when coming from the mouth of a fine woman; and, I am surprized, that as they are excused, from the study of more profound sciences, they do not endeavour to make themselves mistresses, of this kind of merit, which seems indeed, most befitting their sex; as the elegance, and graces of speech, are what is required of them.

THANKS to the *Marquiss*'s invention, this last part of our entertainment, was a little more pleasing, than any of the former had been; but, as there was neither wit, nor good humour, wanting in the four ladies, they did not appear less to me, for being not properly exerted. I said so, to the *Marquiss*, as I carried him home in my coach; he seemed of my opinion,

opinion, but more concerned that it
fhould be fo, as he had lefs delicate ideas
of pleafure; and would at all times,
have preferred *Fanchon*, and her companions, to any virtuous women what-
foever. I added, that I fhould be glad
to fee thefe ladies, but fhould wifh, it
might be in a place, where they might
think themfelves obliged to lefs reftraint, and confequently, put lefs reftraint on thofe, whom they did the
honour to fup with. He was fo defirous of retaining me in this fociety,
that, to engage me to come a third time,
he propofed a new party, and left me
the choice of the evening. This company, *faid he*, will nothing refemble
either of the two former you have feen;
and I am deceived, if you do not find
more fatisfaction in it.

I gave my promife, but could not
prefix a time; which indeed, was more
protracted than I expected, or than he
defired; by fome incidents, which gave
a new face to my fituation. I received
an anfwer from my father to my laft
letter; wherein he told me, that in
compliance

compliance with my requeſt, he had
not only given an account of the declaration, I made to Madamoſelle *de St. V.*
but had alſo engaged her, to read the
letter I had ſent him.---That while ſhe
was thus employed, he thought, he diſcovered emotions in her, of a more violent nature, than thoſe of confuſion or
ſhame. --- That ſhe muſt certainly be a-
gitated by an extreme love, or an extreme hate; that as ſhe ſtill inſiſted on
her firſt pretenſions, after having read
my letter, he believed her capable of
having recourſe, to every thing which
might juſtify them. --- That in regard,
to the explanation I deſired of thoſe con-
deſcentions, ſhe had accuſed herſelf with
on my account; ſhe anſwered in the
utmoſt tranſport of rage, that my demand, was adding inſult to perfidy, and
that, ſhe knew how to do herſelf juſtice, if ſhe was denied it by heaven,
and mankind. ---That her parents complained loudly of the diſhonour I had
brought upon their family; -and that this
adventure was at preſent, the only topic
of converſation round the country.--He
concluded however, with ſaying, that
after

after ſo formal a renounciation, as that
my letter contained, he could not perſuade me any farther; but left me wholly to purſue, what ſeemed beſt to me.

He had reaſon to depend on the juſtice of my heart. — Happineſs and fortune were always too light with me,
when ballanced againſt duty and honour. —I had no difficulty, as to any engagements with this lady, becauſe I was
certain, nothing had eſcaped me, that
could bear that name; but religion and
honour, had laws of a more delicate
nature. Madamoiſelle *de St. V.* ***,
had loſt her reputation, if I did not re-
ſtore it by eſpouſing her: it behoved me,
to examine ſeriouſly, whether through
her own fault, or mine; and the miſ-
fortune being real, and impoſſible to be
repaired, by any other than myſelf;
whether that reparation was not a kind
of duty in me? or, whether on the other
ſide, it exacted from me, the ſacrifice
of my life? for I could look no otherwiſe on a marriage, for which I had no
inclination, than as the worſt of deaths?
— my heart was yet free, — I had been

near

near two months in *Paris*, without
having either miftrefs or friend, though
I had often lamented within myfelf the
want of both; and by what I had heard
of love, or could guefs concerning that
paffion, I had felt fomething which
made me know with what ardour I
could yield to it, if reafon had not hitherto combated my inclination: muft
I then renounce all poffibility of a more
happy occafion to indulge the fweet e-
motion, which I knew not, but in a moment might be prefented to me; to
charge myfelf at this age, with a chain
which I never could be freed from, but by
death; and the weight of which, would
render life a mifery?---*thus did I argue,*
and as *happinefs*, was not capable of
making me betray my *duty*, fo I thought,
I ought, in fuch a dilemma as this,
to be well convinced that it was my *duty* in reality, to forfeit all my hopes of
happinefs. Not being able to determine,
and fearful of being felf-deceived, I bethought me of confulting the opinion
of others, whofe probity could be in no
danger of being influenced by paffion,
as they fhould be fuch as were wholly
difinte-

difintered in the matter, and of whofe
knowledge and underftanding, there was
no doubt to be made.--Where then could
I fo properly addrefs as to M. *M**** ?
I therefore fent my cafe to them, related
naturally as it was, and refolved from
the bottom of my heart, to abide by
their decifion as by the order of heaven.

WHILE I attended their reply, I
fought among all the company I knew,
and in thofe new acquaintance I every
day made, fome means of diffipating the
difquiets of my mind.   One day, a day
which I can never remember without a
mixture of grief and joy, being obliged
to go out on fome bufinefs more early
then was my cuftom ; I paffed by the
door of a church where the great afflu-
ence of people reminding me that it
was a feftival; I ordered my coach to
ftop and went in to hear *mafs*.---I took
a chair juft behind that of a woman,
who feemed intent on her private devo-
tions, till the public fervice began. She
had only one fervant behind her, but
her air made me take her for a perfon
of condition: I fay her air, for it was
by

by that, and the genteelnefs of her pofture, I could as yet alone diftinguifh
her from feveral others who were near
us. Under the moft plain and negli-
gent habit, I found fomething more
noble and more graceful, than I had
ever feen before. I had immediately
the moft ardent curiofity to fee her face,
and fhould have had the boldnefs to
have attempted it, if the confideration
of the place I was in, and the refpect
I thought owing to a woman of her appearance, had not reftrained me.

I could not, however, contain myfelf
till *mafs* was over, but quitting my
place, went to the other fide of the
church, and advancing by little and
little in the fame line, was almoft op-
pofite to her, though yet at too great
a diftance for the fatisfaction of my impatience; on which I ventured two or
three fteps farther, but her head being
turned a little on one fide, had not a
full view of her face: I thought, neverthelefs, that I difcovered features I
had feen before, though I could not

G   prefent-

prefently recollect in what place I had ever beheld any thing fo charming.

The beautiful creature! *cried I to myfelf*. She was without paint, or any ornaments of drefs; but I faw a fkin of the moft dazzling whitenefs; eyes which, without looking on me, pierc'd my very foul; a majefty and mingled fweetnefs of mein, that commanded at once all my love. I admir'd; I a-dor'd; and at laft remembered, that this enchanting perfon was no other than madam *de B* * *, whom I had fupped with at the *Intendant*'s on my arrival in *Paris.*

I was extremely furprized, becaufe the impreffion fhe now made on me was vaftly different from that of the firft view. The reafon of which I afterwards attributed to the red fhe then had on her cheeks, which the ladies of *Paris* affect to wear to an excefs, and very much difgufted me on my firft coming among them; where-

as

as now she appeared only in her native charms, which art could not add to, but disguise.

THE amiable woman! *said I again*, what graces, what admirable qualities are united in that one face? I was indeed too strongly touched with what I saw, and found and checked myself for suffering the thoughts of beauty to interfere with piety, and made an effort to withdraw from the too transporting object. At last I did; yet during the remainder of divine service, could not keep my eyes from glancing that way, while hers, I found, were always intent upon her book, as neither desirous of attracting, nor knowing she did so.

HER unworthy attachment to her husband's clerk then came into my head, and in spite of the pleasure it gave me to look upon her, I was now shock'd at such an appearance of devotion, which could be called no other than the most base hypocrisy. Yet,

G 2 *said*

said I to myself, is there not a possibility for this amiable woman to be injured by cruel reports, as I have already found many others have been? Is not the world full of scandal and barbarity, and in particular fond of blasting real merit.

This consideration gave me a moment's pleasure; but then again the accusations against her seemed too well founded, to afford me any lasting comfort. They were in a manner proved by the nature of the circumstances, and even by the effects. Why else that obstinacy in staying continually at home? Why does she shun all conversation, and fly even her best and most intimate friends? Is it likely that a woman of her age, born to please, should be able to despise all that has charms for youth and beauty, and chuse to live the life of a Recluse?

These imaginations diminished great part of that impression the sight of her had

had made on me.   I fupped that night
with madam the *Intendant*, and told
her not only that I had feen madam
de B * * at church, but alfo the new
admiration from which I could not defend myfelf.

THIS Lady, after having acknowledged the charms of the perfon I mentioned, fell again, with her former feverity, on the capricioufnefs of her
paffion.   I eafily difcovered fhe was
piqued at the other's refraining her vifits;
but I could not think that was a fufficient motive for blafting her reputation.
Befides, I had heard the fame from o-
thers : they faid the clerk was young
and handfome, her husband full of infirmities, and that at her years, and in
her fituation, the amufement fhe
gave herfelf, could fcarce be called a
crime.

SEVERAL days paffed over without
my thinking of madam *de B* * *, but
to be forry for her ill conduct : in the
mean time, I received an anfwer to my

G 3   problem

problem of honour and religion, and found it such as I had hoped, and which I should not have hesitated one moment to have given myself to any other person; my uncertainty having only proceeded from that excess of e-quity, if I may so call it, which always made me fearful of judging in my own cause.

I was extremely pleased, however, to have my opinion ratified by the most judicious, and most virtuous men in *Paris*. I very much pitied madam-moiselle *de St. V* * *, but had not the least disquiet for the effect of her hate, as my father seemed to apprehend. The joy of finding myself delivered from this dilemma, made me the more readily agree to the old *Marquiss*'s pro-posals.

THEY had several suppers, where he told me, my absence had been much re-gretted; and to justify his fondness for the entertainments of those private pleasure-houses, he had been eight days in pro-curing

curing a company, such as I should
have nothing to object against. And
I then engaged to make one of so a-
greeable a party, at the time he appointed.

DURING this interval, there happened to me three incidents, all which
I should acknowledge as favours from
heaven, if the last of them had not, till
even this day, been mingled with troubles which will not suffer me to give it
that name. It gave birth, indeed, to
all the happiness of my life, but it has
been the occasion of all my sorrows and
disgraces.

AFTER having ruin'd, for fifteen
years, my repose and my fortune, it has
exposed, within these six months, my
head to the last danger; and though a
friend, too generous and too tender,
has preserved my life at the expence of
very near losing his own, it has only
made me fall by other adventures into
a situation, where all the consolation
of my misfortunes is the liberty of

G 4   writing

writing them: Neverthelefs, in the midft of my melancholly reflections, my memory fometimes prefents me, with the Images of thofe bleffings, which preceded my pains; and which, will be ever dear to me, in fpite of the ill fate, that deprives me of the reality.

THE *Prefident de* ****, for whom I had the greateft efteem, perceived with pleafure, the defire I had to cultivate a friendfhip with him; and would frequently when full of company, find opportunity of difcourfing with me alone, on fubjects more ferious, than he found many of thofe, who vifited him, were defirous of being engaged in.

YOU are formed, *faid he to me one day*, to be well looked upon, in all forts of focieties; I find, you give pleafure wherever you come, but I fcarce believe, you take the fame yourfelf, with fome at leaft, of thofe you converfe with. I am certain, you would think yourfelf much more happy in many families,

families, whom I have inspired with a desire of being known to you; and I must, some day or another, introduce you.

I assured him, with a great deal of sincerity, that I should always be ready to follow so excellent a conductor. --He then desired, I would dine with him the same day, at a house, where he often visited. As I had no engagement, I accepted the offer, and sent away my coach, in order to accompany him, in his chariot.

As we were going, I will not attempt to prejudice you, *said he*, in favour of the persons to whom I shall present you; but leave you to judge, according to what proportion of merit you shall find in them. . I will only tell you, that it is with such as these, I pass the hours of real life; for I look on the entertainments I receive in some houses, no better than the idle amusements of a dream.

This, was however, sufficient to inform

form me, of the characters of those,
I was going to be introduced to; and
there passed little more, till we arrived
at the door, of a very fine house.--The
President, made me enter without ceremony; and seemed no less free than at
home. We found, in an apartment
richly furnished, five or six persons, to
whom he presented me. This, *said he,
to him who seemed to be the master*, is
Monsieur the *Count de ***; I have
spoke to you of his merit, and to him,
of the desire you have of knowing him.

After the first compliments, we
all sat down, and, the very beginning
of the conversation, discovered to me
two things, which since my being in
Paris, were perfectly new to me.---An
innocent vivacity, which produced pleasantry without disorder; and a judici-
ousness, which is the effect of learning,
wit, knowledge of the world, and good
taste united.

At first, I had some guard over myself,

felf, left any thing fhould efcape me,
'unworthy of the company I was among;
but I foon found, I had no occafion for
reftraint with perfons, who were no
lefs eafy in their manners, than juft in
their ideas. — All they faid, was elegant
and full of truth; but without the leaft
mixture of felf-fufficiency, or affectation. None feemed eager to fpeak, or
defirous of being filent: they liftened
with complaifance, and anfwered with.
fincerity: wit, good humour, knowledge and politenefs, came together from
the fame mouth: no difcourfes appeared more plain, or more fweet, yet none
could convey more improvement to
the mind. In fine, all human merits,
with all human pleafures, feemed to
be here affembled.——Men and women of the fame principles, fame tafte,
fame manners, with good chear, good
wine, and every thing elfe that could
regale the underftanding, or the fenfes.

I N going out of this houfe, I told
the *Prefident* that after the happinefs
I had quitted, no other anxiety remained

ed upon me, but the fears of not being able to re-enjoy it ; for it seems to
me, *said I*, as if the soul of merit,
had here shut itself up as in a temple,
inacceffable to all who had not equal
talents.

WERE your high idea real, *replied
the* President *with a smile*, it would
certainly be always open to you.----I
perceive so much of the good impression you have left behind, as to venture to affure you, that you cannot go
there too often. Though my admiration of all this company in general
was very great ; yet I cannot but say,
there was one whose phisiognomy and
manners particularly charmed me. He
seemed to be about thirty years of age,
and wit, elegance, good taste and good
humour, were as natural to him, as to
breathe.

THE *President* told me he was called Monsieur *de la* * * * *, and that being the eldest of a very honourable family, he had quitted the service since the
death

death of his father.   On my expreſs-
ing a deſire of ſeeing him again, for
I found he was only a viſitor where
we had been, he told him I might depend on it, not only at the ſame place,
but alſo at ſeveral others where he intended to preſent me.

WHAT, *cried I,* are there any other
houſes reſembling this we came from?
this doubt, *anſwered he,* proves more
than ever to me, that you yet know
little of *Paris,* and that you judge of
all aſſemblies by thoſe I firſt happened
to ſee you at.----The family we have
juſt quitted, *added he,* is certainly extremely amiable, and there are few
which can excel them in all the good
qualities, either of mind or body; yet
you will find a great number, allow-
ing for the difference of degree, who
have the ſame principles, and obſerve
the ſame rules.

I liſtened eagerly to what he ſaid,
and nothing but the great confidence I
had in him, could have perſuaded me
                                         to

to give credit to it.-----So difficult are
our firſt prejudices to be eradicated! I
did not quit him, till he had given me
repeated aſſurances of eſtabliſhing me
in this ſociety of *true merit*, for ſo I
chuſe to call this laſt, in oppoſition to
thoſe others I had been among, where
I had ſeen corruption, and the falſe maxims of the world, ſo triumphant over
juſtice, true reaſon, and virtue. I could
not compare the one with the other,
without indignation, at that air of preſumption which I found ſo predomi-
nant, nor reflect without a mixture of
contempt and pity, on the wretched
abuſe of birth and riches, by perſons
who made them only the cover of ill-
nature, and ignorance.

I went home ſo little diſpoſed to continue my acquaintance, with the greateſt part of thoſe I had been accuſtomed to ſup with, that having ſome letters to write, I paſt the evening alone
in my own apartment. Theſe reflections I had carried to bed with me, en-
groſſed my mind for a good part of the
night

night, which occafioned my fleeping
fomewhat longer than was my cuftom
in the morning.   On my waking I was
told that Monfieur *de la* * * * *, that
fame perfon of whom I had fpoken
with fo much efteem to the *Prefident*,
had been fome minutes in my anti-
chamber.   Finding that I was yet in
bed, but that it was near the hour of
my rifing, he would not fuffer my people to difturb me, and waited till my
bell gave notice I was willing to be vi-
fible.   The impatience I had to receive
him, made me renounce the ceremony of drefs.----I threw on my night-
gown, and flew out of my chamber:
he ran with open arms to meet me,
and the compliment he made me was,
that of a perfon who to a perfect knowledge of the world, had joined in him
the amiable principles of goodnefs and
tendernefs of heart.   He had been informed by the Prefident, *he told me*,
of the fentiments I had conceived in
his favour, and having found the fame
difpofition in himfelf towards me, he
could not refift coming immediately to
testifie

teftifie the double emotions of his inclination and his gratitude.----I come,
added he embracing me, to defire your
friendfhip and efteem, and to offer the
fame on my part during my   whole
life.

I now felt an impreffion which made
me know, that friendfhip for a worthy
perfon, is a paffion little lefs powerful
than that which is called love, when
infpired by one of a different fex. I
returned his embrace with ardency.
I give you nothing, *anfwered I*, fince
your merit has acquired all that you
afk of me with fo good a grace : but
I will confirm, by all the affurances
that ftricteft truth and honour can dic-
tate, that I can refufe nothing to prove
myfelf devoted to you.   In fine, we
were fo perfectly fatisfied with each o-
ther, that our converfation immediately
became as familiar, as that of perfons who had been intimates for a long
time.

THO*

Tho' sympathy is looked upon as a chimera, by those whose rougher minds allows them not the happiness of proving its reality, monsieur *de La* * * *, without my requesting it, found that he should do me a pleasure in communicating to me his situation. He told me, that being the eldest of his family, with a brother and two sisters, who were yet scarce out of their infancy, he thought he might be dispensed with for leaving the service, in order to supply the place of their father to them: that he had caused them to be brought to *Paris*, that they might be brought up under his own eye, in the house of a near kinswoman, a woman, *said he*, ill defended from the censure of the world herself, by the unhappiness of being separated from her husband, but endowed with so much good sense and virtue, as renders her justly amiable to all persons capable of judging; she is called, *added he*, the marchioness *de N* * *.

This being the very lady whom, by the account given by Madame, the
wife

wife of our *Intendant*, I had more
than once called the marchionels of three
lovers, I could not forbear uttering
fomething that founded like an exclamation in the firft motion of my indignation, as well as my furprize.

MONSEUR *de La* * * *, finding himfelf interrupted, was at a lofs to comprehend the reafon; on which I entreated him to continue his difcourfe,
promifing to give him hereafter the
explanation of that aftonifhment I had
betrayed.

ON this he continued to tell me,
that having nothing of importance to
relate to me, his fole defign in entertaining me in this manner, was to
fhew, that he would have no referve
towards me. That befides the houfe
where we had dined together the day
before, there were feveral others in
which he flattered himfelf with the
hope of meeting me, when I was
made fenfible of the defire they had to
be made acquainted with me: that for
example

example of his cousin, the *Marchioness*,
he could assure me deserved, I should
sometimes take the pains to enter.   I
am impatient, *said he*, till I introduce
you to that lady, who though very
much afflicted at being parted from a
husband whom she married through
inclination, yet has not her good nature or understanding the least impair-
ed by the trouble of her mind.

HER life indeed has been a scene of
sorrows; the ill usage of her unworthy
husband obliged her to quit him, and
in order to purchase that liberty, con-
signed over to him a good part of her
revenue; but being abandoned to all
kinds of excess and debauchery, he
attempted, by every kind of violence
in his power, to extort from her an
augmentation of his pension; and had
infallibly forced her to it, even to the
depriving herself of the necessary ap-
pointments of a woman of quality, if
myself, and two other friends, had not
stood up in her defence; which has so
incensed him, that too abject spirited to
resent

refent his difapointment as becomes a
man of honour, he has recourfe to the
moft infamous calumnies, publifhing,
wherever he comes, that his wife has
no lefs than three gallants. But fecure
in her innocence, fhe defpifes thofe ridiculous reports, which are only fhameful to thofe who give credit to them
without proof, and thinks the efteem
of thofe who truly know her, fufficient
to balance againft the ill opinion of thofe
who do not.

I heard monfieur continue his difcourfe on this head without interpofing
one word; but when I perceived he
had done, I told him that I believed I
had known the marchionefs before, not
in the picture he gave me of her, but
in fuch a one as malice and injuftice
had drawn out.

Such is the misfortune of the fex,
replied he, beauty and merit always
attracts envy, and if women, poffeft of
fuch qualities, happen to fall into any
adventure that makes a noife in the
world,

world, it is sure to be represented in all the bad colours that barbarity can find. I do not however wish, *continued he*, that you would depend on the character I have given, but that you will favour us with your company at dinner, that you may know her better.

As there appeared no occasion for ceremony, with a person so nearly allied to him, I readily yielded to attend him; but, as the confidence he had reposed in me, demanded the same on my part; I entered into the detail of my affairs, particularly, that of Madamoiselle *de St. V* * * *, and was rejoiced, to find his judgment agree with that of *M. de M.* * *. After this, we fell on the inhumanity of scandal, and the little dependance, ought to be placed on public rumour.

The proof I was going to receive of the injustice had been done to the *Marchioness*, made me reflect, there was a possibility, that Madame *de B* * *, might also suffer, from that cruel spirit
of

of envy and detraction. This imagination grew so strong upon me, that
presently, I accused myself, for having
ever given way, to any suspicions of
her innocence. What, *said I to myself*,
can such an appearance of the perfect
modesty and discretion, serve only for
the mask, of the most shameful weakness? can so charming a body, be af-
sociated with a mind, deformed with
vice? it seemed to me, even by the
rules of physick, that such an accord,
was impossible in nature; for the lines
of the face, are for the most part, the
signification of the heart.

CAN a violent grief, be disguised in
a perpetual smile? none will pretend it
can. Then how can an irregular, an
unlawful passion, be concealed under a
constant shew of innocence and modesty? — I fancied, while my thoughts
were thus pleading the cause of that
beautiful person, it was only my love of
justice and truth, that furnished me
with arguments, nor should have difcovered that my heart was interested
by

by other secret reasons. I had not dis-
coursed of it with those emotions, which
are natural to the passion I was possest
of, to a friend for whom, I did not wish
to have any reserve.

I knew not before, that the *Marchi-*
oness lived in the same street with madame the *Intendant*, but I now found
that the near neighbourhood between
them, rather than any friendship on
either side, had brought them acquainted.——We were seven at dinner, five
men with a lady of much the same
age with the *Marchioness*, that is to
say, about thirty-two, or thirty-three
years: and I was soon convinced I
might depend on the judgment of Monsieur *de la* *** by the satisfaction I
found in this little circle.——They were
all of the same principles, and same
manners with those I had dined with
the preceeding day; and in a very few
hours had those sentiments concerning
the character of the *Marchioness*, which
he had foretold I should on conversing
with her. On my mentioning the *In-*
tendant's

tendant's lady, fhe remembered fhe had
feen me at her houfe ; but *faid fhe,*
I do not often vifit there, becaufe I
make a wide diftinction between friends
and acquaintance, and have no real pleafure in life, but with the former.

I then could not forbear mentioning
madame *De B * * *,* who had fupped
with us the fame night, hoping that by
drawing a woman of fo much good
fenfe as the *Marchionefs* into fome difcourfe of hers, I might be able to have
my doubts cleared up ; but fhe only
faid, that lady feldom went abroad. So
fhort an anfwer very much perplexed
me ; however, to engage her to be more
explicit if poffible, I added, that I had
heard very odd reafons given for her
ftaying fo much at home. Alafs ! *replied the Marchionefs,* what will not envy fuggeft ! there are people who will
not be perfuaded, that a woman can be
difcreet with youth and beauty. ———
Knowing Madame *de B * * *,* fo little
as I do, I cannot judge if the reports
fpread concerning her, be true or falfe;
but

but I am not eaſy to believe any thing,
againſt a woman, who appears ſo amiable; and am of the opinion, that there
are many more malicious tongues, than
deceitful countenances.

I perceived it was not from this lady,
I was to receive any deciſion, prejudicial
to the reputation of another. There
was notwithſtanding, an air of uncertainty in her reply, which ſhewed me,
to what a pitch the public opinion,
was declared againſt Madam *de B* * * *.
I could not for all this, but oppoſe the
blindneſs of prejudice: in all that I had
heard, I could not find any proof a-
gainſt her; and I thought, that both
good ſenſe, and good nature, ought to
reject all accuſations, that had not a reſemblance of truth. — In a word, the
deſire of being convinced of the virtue
of that beautiful woman, became a
kind of paſſion in me; but what hope
was there of my being ſo ? the *Marchi-
oneſs* propoſed *Quadrille*, and I engaged
in it with the more willingneſs, as I
was not in a fit diſpoſition for diſcourſe.

H

But the following night, my reflections grew more serious than ever, on the state of my affairs. As my acquaintance at *Paris* increased, I had laid down a plan to be as happy as I could, in all the different companies I came among: on a strict examination into myself, I found I was made more for pleasure than fortune; but in a time when there was no prospect of war, or at least, a very distant one, I thought I might be excused, for not listening to ambition; and I was enough content with the estate I was in possession of, which I knew, would also be considerably augmented at the death of my father, not to wish any accession to it. The extreme desire I always had, for the society of worthy persons, made me give thanks to heaven, for those recent advantages the *President* had procured for me. As he perfectly understood true merit, and loved it, I doubted not, but these first proofs he had given me, of his discernment in that point, would be succeeded by others; for virtue is not steril, where one vein is discovered;

covered; we are sure of finding, as in
mines of metal, a communication with
a great number : I had already drawn
from this rich source, the most precious of all earthly treasures, an amiable and virtuous friend, whose esteem
I was resolved to cultivate by all the
means in my power.

WHAT, indeed, was now wanting
to render me completely happy ? I
had sufficient to employ either my
serious, or my gayer hours, and to
leave no void in time. The duties
my birth and station in the world required of me, such as appearing among
the great, and paying my respects to
those who had been my father's friends;
the gratifying my inclination for pleasure, in beholding public shews, being
present at all great festivals, operas,
balls, comedies, and sometimes even
at those private suppers as the *Marquifs* called them, not excepting those
where all manner of liberties were allowed : all this, joined with the study
of that science I had embraced, and
the necessity there was for me some-

times

times of joining the regiment, one would
imagine fhould have left me nothing to
wifh or to regret.

YET was I agitated with ftrange difquiets, and felt fomething within my
mind to which I could not give a
name. The vifit I had made to the
marchionefs *de N* **, had not only ab-
folutely deftroyed all the falfe impreffions which the *Intendant* had given me on her fcore, but had alfo
ftrengthened the hope I had of finding
madam *de B**** no lefs innocent; but
as it did not amount to an affurance fhe
was fo, I was refolved, at any rate, to
fatisfy a curiofity, which I thought,
had nothing guilty in it. After a thoufand inventions for that purpofe, I fixed on one which afforded me a rea-
fonable profpect of fuccefs : which was
this.

I fent to *Sedan* for my quarter-
mafter, in order, as I pretended, to
raife me fome dragoons, which I found
were wanting in my troop. He was
a *Parifen*, a man of a good deal of
ex-

experience and difcretion. I charged him to take a lodging in the fame ftreet with madam *de B****, to make himfelf acquainted in the neighbour-hood, and to find out in what manner fhe lived with her hufband; how fhe amufed herfelf, and what were the motives which made her fhun the con-verfation of the world, and avoid vi-fiting or being vifited. This feemed to me the moft probable way of coming at the truth, becaufe there are few things done in any family, without being reported by fome one or other of the domeftics.

My quarter-mafter carried his zeal to oblige me, fomewhat too far. In two days after I had given him my commands, he came to me with an air of the utmoft fatisfaction in his face, told me he had got acquainted with the clerk of monfieur *de B****, and that having engaged him to drink, had prevailed on him to enter himfelf a dragoon in my company; but, *faid* he had avoided fpeaking to him concern-ing madam *de B****, becaufe he

H 3 thought

thought it would be more in my own power to draw from him an account of every thing I defired to know.

I was feized with the moft violent rage on hearing this : What have you done, *cried I?* you have given a mortal difquiet to the moft amiable of all womankind. Never! never! will fhe forgive it. This exclamation efcaped me, without reflecting on what I faid, and I even added to it other extravagancies, as if the difobliging a woman I fo little knew, was a matter of the greateft importance in life to me ; however, as my paffion abated, I began to look on this adventure with a different eye.

I wanted to be fatisfied, and there could not be a more certain way of being fo : if madam *de B* * * * was in reality the flave of a vile propenfity, I found a fecret pleafure in curing her of it, by removing the object out of her fight ; and if fhe had been unjuftly accufed, befides the joy of finding her

inno-

innocent, I fhould have the honour of conferring an obligation on her by releafing the clerk from his engagement.

I did not examine from what fource thefe reafonings proceeded, and only defired the new dragoon might be brought to me that fame moment: but he having defired permiffion to return to his mafter that night, in order to fettle his affairs, he was gone home, and I could not fee him till the next day.

I had little repofe that night, and on my rifing, called ten times to know if the clerk was yet come ; and noon drawing on without his appearing, my quarter-mafter, who began to grow uneafy at his abfence, was going in fearch of him, when word was brought me, that a footman from madam *de* B * * * attended with a letter for me. Here was fubject of frefh emotion for me ! however, I eafily conceived that the clerk, after the fumes of the wine were diffipated, had repented what he

had

had done, and confeffed his folly to his
mafter: on which madam *de B * * **,
finding I was the captain, had wrote
to me to obtain his liberty.

I opened the letter with an agitation
not to be defcribed, and found I had
not been deceived in my conjectures. It
was a moft preffing folicitation in favour
of a poor young man, *fhe faid*, who
was not addicted to any vicious courfes,
and that it was, doubtlefs, only the
force of liquor, which had engaged
him in a party no way convenient for
him. She reminded me of the fupper
where we both were, at madam the
Intendant's, becaufe, *fhe faid*, it was
poffible her name might not have
flipped my memory; and left it to myfelf what ranfom fhould be paid
for the difcharge of her hufband's
clerk.

I read this letter four times over:
I obferved the ftile and manner with
the utmoft exactnefs; but in fpite of
the extreme defire I had to find her
innocent, a thoufand cruel fufpicions
of

of her guilt rofe in my mind. I
thought there was an air of tendernefs in the expreffions fhe made ufe of,
which muft be dictated by paffion,
———*a poor young man*; how kind,
cried I, fhe laments him! She loves
him! She is befotted! ——— then
leaving me to name the fum, as if fhe
thought nothing too much for his re-
demption. What could fhe do more
for a hufband, or a brother? The
grief thefe ideas inflicted on me, did
not, however, hinder me from feizing
the opportunity of obliging her, of
feeing her, and judging with my own
eyes, of her conduct and fentiments;
and, to that end, bid her footman be
told, I would receive his miftrefs's
commands in perfon.

BUT as this was not a vifit of form,
but bufinefs, I thought I might be
difpenfed with from mentioning the
hour. The truth is, I was willing to
furprize her, fo that without giving
her time to prepare herfelf, I dreffed
that inftant, and went directly to the
houfe of monfieur *de B* * * * : on my
telling

telling my name at the door, I perceived an extraordinary confufion among the fervants, which made me conclude, the favour of the lady had rendered the clerk a perfon of fuch importance, that all interefted themfelves in his fate. He prefently appeared himfelf, very dejected and fearful.

HE was about eighteen or twenty years of age, his fhape and ftature were tolerable, but his vifage was long, his features far from agreeable, with a very fwarthy complexion, and his hair behind his ears, as clerks commonly wear it. He difcovered fo little fpirit in his eyes, that I was half eafed of my doubts, yet could not help faying to him, with a little fpite, that he had nothing to fear from his engagement for the fervice of the king, if madam *de B* *** was refolved to continue him in hers. Could a fellow, fuch as this, *cried I, as I was going up*, think of turning his back on the moft charming woman in the world!

As

As I was not expected so soon, madam had not opportunity to throw off her domestic habit, but it was neat, and becoming a modest woman, who always charms most, when she least thinks of doing it. She received me with an air of confusion, which, instead of taking from her beauty, only served to add to it. And after having agreeably reproached me with an excess of politeness, for the trouble I had given myself, entreated me to pass into a neighbouring chamber, where her husband was lying languishing in his bed.

See, *said she*, monsieur, the *count de* ———, has prevented the civilities he might expect from us ; but the condition you are in, I flatter myself, will plead our pardon ; and, I doubt not, but it has already done so, by his adding to the favour we entreated, the honour of a visit.

I assured them both, with a great deal of truth, that if I had any part
in

in an affair which had been so dis-
obliging to them, I should have thought
it impossible any excuses I could make
sufficient atonement.

I then explained to them, that my
quarter-master had gone beyond the
bounds I ordered, which were only to
enter such young men as were entirely
out of business; and when I had ended, presented a discharge for the clerk,
to the hands of madam *de B* ***, but
she refused to accept it, till I had named the sum at which I set his liberty. O! madam, *said I, tearing it in
pieces*, you little know my character or
disposition.

This facility in parting with my
dragoon, destroyed all my designs;
which were, indeed, to find how far
her good-will extended to this young
man, by the price she would be willing to pay for him; but I was sway-
ed by the force of an ascendant, which
would not permit me to make such a
trial. Besides, I was willing to give
this proof of my disinterestedness, and
that

that I preferred the esteem of worthy persons, to any venal considerations. I doubt not but I also wished
she might discover something in my
behaviour of a zeal infinitely beyond
what is to be found in an ordinary politeness : but these were sentiments,
which, how just soever, I did not think
I entertained at that time.

THE tone and manner in which I
spoke, convincing her, that she could
not make a second offer of composi-
tion without affronting the delicacy of
my generosity ; neither she, nor her
husband attempted it, but gave me a
thousand testimonies of their gratitude
and esteem. The conversation after
became more familiar. I asked her
husband what were his infirmities, and
he told me, that the labour of his stu-
dies, on account of his profession, joined with a weak constitution, had thrown
him, for near a year ago, into a deep
consumption ; that his appetite and repose being entirely destroyed, he had
continued wasting every day more and
more, and for three or four months,

I   had

had not been able to quit his bed. After having condoled his misfortune, *I
said*, the unhappy state you are in,
will admit no consolation but the society of a dear and amiable wife, who
seems to have declared war with the
world, that she may not lose a moment
of your company.

He was touched with these words,
even to shedding some tears; Alas!
answered he, the praises of a wife,
sound but ill from the mouth of a husband; but if Madame did not hear me,
I would give you her character, as the
prodigy of her sex. She merits all the
satisfactions are to be found in marriage,
and I despair of ever seeing her partake
any thing but the pains. To this she
made a reply, no less tender than modest, but had not ended it when he interrupted her by saying, I am continually pressing her to take those diversions,
which are agreeable to her age; yet,
does she obstinately refuse all sollicita-
tions on that score. This little chamber
is the world to her. Here she sits, from
morning till night, either at work, or
reading

reading to me, never quitting me, but to go into that closet, where she has made her bed be placed; so, on hearing the least noise, she immediately comes to me, and offers me those services, which she would be sorry I should receive from any other hand.

But I shall die with less regret, *added he*, because my death in spite of her, will put her into a situation, more worthy of her merit and her virtue. Madame *de B.* * * *, made a second reply, more natural if possible, than the former; and, in spite of the diffidence which I might have, concerning the credulity of a Man, deprived of one half of his senses, I could not resist giving credit, to what came out of so beautiful a mouth. They made the clerk come in to return his thanks, for the freedom I had bestowed upon him; and the timid and submissive manner, in which he received the compliments his lady told him were my due, yet more weakened my suspicions concerning him; and when she told me, he was discended from no very mean family, and had been recommended to her husband, as

a

a young man of fober inclinations, I
heard this praife with lefs pain, than I
had read thofe in the letter.

FAR from confidering, that the
length of my vifit might be incommo-
dious to them, or being uneafy myfelf,
at the company of a fick man, I utterly
forgot how the time paffed away. Monfieur *de B.* * * * took notice, that I was
not difpleafed with his converfation,
nor with that of his wife ; my countenance it feems, did me that good office,
if I could hope, *faid he*, that in compaffion to Madame *de B.* * *, you would
fometimes venture to come, and breathe
the ill air of a fick man's chamber, I
fhould be very preffing to obtain that
favour. While he was fpeaking this,
I difcovered fome kind of confufion, in
the eyes of his wife ; he obferved it alfo, and afked her, if fhe would not be
glad I fhould pafs with them that time
which he muft confefs, I could not
worfe employ, though in a charitable
intent ? you may be fure *anfwered fhe*,
I fhall always fhare in the pleafure you
will take, at feeing Monfieur the *Count*
here ; and am only perplexed, at the
pennance

pennance he muſt lay upon himſelf, in
complying with your requeſt. But the
world, *added ſhe after a pauſe*, is a cen-
ſor extremely dangerous. Thoſe that
know you, *replied her husband, with a
more than ordinary vivacity*, will be
forced to reſpect you; and of importance to you, are the judgments of thoſe
who know you not? beſides, in this affair, malice would be ridiculous as well
as blind. As it was my cauſe, which
this gallant ſick perſon was pleading with
ſo much warmth, I could not but ſecond him, by aſſuring Madame *de B.* *,
that my behaviour ſhould be ſuch, as
would juſtify the favours I received, either
from Monſieur or herſelf.

THE delicious tranſports which thril-
led my very ſoul, at commencing this
acquaintance, made me know, that
Madame *de B.* * *, was extremely dear
to me; but I could not diſtinguiſh what
it was I wiſhed, or, with what I would
be ſatisfied. I thought it ſo impoſſible,
that I ſhould ever be poſſeſt of any o-
ther ſentiments, than thoſe of eſteem
and friendſhip for a woman already
engaged in the ſacred ties of marriage,
K   that

that I did not even attempt to defend myself either against her charms, or the weakness of my own heart. I had however, gained two advantages, with which at first, I was highly delighted. The first was the power of undeceiving the *Intendant*'s lady, and all those who had the same prejudices; but then, I remembred how ill I had succeeded in the same enterprize, on the score of the *Financier*, kinsman to the *Marquiss de ***, and I was unwilling to venture a second rebuff. The world is not only unjust in its judgments, but blind and violent in maintaining them; as if the shame of having been in an error, were worse than the obstinacy of defending it. This is indeed the height of cruelty, but the practice is verified by experience. As to the second, the permission of visiting Monsieur *de B ***, I was resolved to use it with a discretion, which should not expose the honour of his wife, to new outrages; and therefore let two days pass over, without presenting myself.

END of the First PART.

MEMOIRS

OF A

MAN

OF

HONOUR.

Translated from the *French.*

PART II.

L O N O N:

Printed for John Nourse, over-againſt
Katherine-ſtreet in the *Strand.*

MDCCXLVII.

MEMOIRS

OF A

MAN *of* HONOUR.

PART II.

NEVERTHELESS I forgot not towards evening, that I was under another engagement with the old *Marquiſs*; and, at the time appointed, went to the chevalier's receſs of pleaſure, the way to which began to grow familiar to me; but it was now civility and complaiſance alone that carried me. For after having been twice deceived by the *Marquiſs*, I could not promiſe myſelf much amuſement the third time.

THE

THE firſt company I had ſeen without eſteem, and the third without pleaſure, and I believed the whole ſcene exhauſted. I imagined that the fair ſex were comprized in the two claſſes of honeſt women and proſtitutes, and could not conceive a poſſibility of there being a third.

THE company were already aſ- ſembled: the men were very near the ſame as before; as for the women, there was two of the moſt celebrated actreſſes at the opera, with two other very fine perſons: the one, miſtreſs of a director of the *India* company, who had em- barked for the *Eaſt* two days before, on the account of his merchandize; the other belonged to a gentleman of the long robe, who that morning had been ſeized with a fit of the gout.

I found the joyful band going out of the hall into the garden, and was preſented to the ladies as a man of quality, rich, and who had not been inſpired with any ſentiments of tender- neſs

nefs for their fex fince my arrival at
Paris.   O! that is quite new indeed!
cried Madamoifelle X. one of the two ac-
treffes, and addreffing herfelf to me with
an air of the utmoft gaiety, 'tis for us,
monfieur, that you have referved your
heart.   Come, come! my chains, *continued fhe, turning her voice into a
graver at that word,* have an enchanting fweetnefs in them.   *Madammoi-
felle* XI. the other actrefs, ftopped me
by the arm, and *faid in the fame tone
and quavering alfo in the laft word,*
No, no, monfieur, that is a conqueft
of which I muft difpute the glory.
That fame inftant *Madamoifelle* XII.
miftrefs of the *Director,* advanced o-
ver-againft me, and made me a polite
compliment, but with fomewhat lefs
freedom.   *Madamoifelle* XIII. miftrefs
of the gentleman of the long robe, did
not give her time to finifh, before fhe
accofted me in her turn, and I could
not help wondering, that the title of a
man arrived but two months, fhould
make thefe four wantons fo impatient
of engaging him.

I affected the fame apifhnefs, and anfwered them fucceffively in the fame
order, and with the fame quavers. I
faid to the firft, that it was love himfelf that had referved me for her cha-
ti-ai-ai-aines, and that I already felt the
fweetnefs of them : to the fecond, that
having a heart capable of rendering a
double facrifice to love, fhe need not
difpute my conqueft, too happy in adding to her glo-o-o-o-ry ; to the third,
that I was not of an age, to make any
difference between two and three; to
the fourth, that if fhe would accept me
divided between four, fhe fhould find me
like a ferpent, whofe each part when
cut to pieces, retains its life and fenfi-
bility.

THIS beginning, which was carried
on with a multitude of other fallies of
gaiety and fpirit, put us all into the moft
pleafant humour can be imagined; and,
was fo far from flagging, that it increafed
every moment. The women had more
wit than I expected : I do not mean,
that fort of wit, which is the effect of
thought;

thought, and reflection, judgment or
the power of reafoning : what they faid
had nothing of all thefe. How fhall
one define it then ? can there be an effect
without a caufe ? their difcourfes had nothing in them, from nothing proceeded,
nor nothing aimed at ; yet did they, for
a whole long night, keep up the fpirit
of inceffant mirth, and joy ; fo, that
if what they faid was nothing, it was
certainly, the moft agreeable nothing in
the world.

As to their perfons, each had her
peculiar merit. *Madamoifelle X.* was a
little fair woman, well fhaped, and had,
in two fmall blue eyes, a fufficient ftock
of fire, to have rendered twice the
number fparkling. All her motions,
were full of vivacity and fprightlinefs,
her fpeech the fame, and could not
come out of a more beautiful mouth :
fhe fung as fhe fpoke, intirely uncon-
ftrained, and with an air of wagifhnefs ;
her voice was not extremely loud, but
foft, and perfectly clear.

THE figure of *Madamoiselle* XI. would never have made a conqueſt of me ; for, however, ſome people may admire ſuch features, a great head, with a very narrow forehead, and a picked chin, had no charms for me : ſhe was alſo very indifferently ſhaped, though they aſſured me it was only being grown more plump ; I thought her, however, too thick and ſhort ; but ſhe atoned for her ill make, by the agreeableneſs of her humour, and the turn ſhe gave to every thing ſhe ſaid : ſhe ſeemed to have an exhauſtleſs ſource to furniſh converſation with (what I call) pleaſing nothings, but which excite, not only laughter in the face, but mirth at the heart.

AFTER having borne much more than her part in a pleaſantry of ſix or ſeven hours together, ſhe took it into her head to continue it in a new manner, and ſung a great number of little catches, in a voice indeed ſomewhat lower than the other, but with an infinity of humour.

IN

In point of beauty, *Madamoiselle* XII. very much excelled all the other three. Few faces had more regular features, or could boast a finer complexion. Her hair, her shape, and mein, had also their peculiar graces. As to vivacity, she had less than either of the two former, but yet enough to animate her discourse by the help of example, and the wine of *Champaigne*. She affected, however, to meditate on what she was about to say, and as our conversation was all light and trifling, an air of study took off great part of the spirit, and though at first I had the better opinion of her judgment, I soon found myself mistaken, and when she became more free, it did not become her better. They told me she had inspired her lover with so violent a passion for her, that he had four times fallen into a fever on the necessity of parting with her, and that he had obliged her to constancy by the most unheard of oaths. She confessed to us, that she had taken them with readiness enough, but repented of them the next morning, and was not sure she should e-

ven

ven remember them the next day. She could not sing, but danced with an admirable grace, and she took care to improve that talent, as she imagined it might be a resource against any reverse in life, by rendering her acceptable in the opera-house.

AT the first look *Madamoiselle* XIII. was only pretty, but to those that saw her for a quarter of an hour, she appeared more beautiful. There was a kind of magic in her eyes, which diffused a thousand charms over all her person. She had a very white neck, and a clear complexion, but not one regular feature; nothing but that undiscribable brightness, which issued from two eyes, the finest and most tender in the world, could have made any harmony between things which seemed formed never to be found together. A large mouth, for example, and teeth of a most surprizing smallness; a short nose, and yet sharp; a narrow forehead, with broad temples; huge arms, and the most diminitive hands I ever saw: yet the look with which she accompanied

companied every ſmile, rendered her enchanting.   The lips of this great mouth
were of the fineſt vermillion ; the little
teeth were even, and of an admirable
whiteneſs : upon that low forehead grew
hair of an excellent colour, and in great
order ; and the wide temples ſeemed
extended only to ſhew the beauty of the
blue ſerpentine veins. I never beheld any
thing ſo ſpiteful as the little noſe which
turned itſelf up towards the eyes, as if
to rob them of their ſhine.   In fine, the
childiſh hands at the end of arms quite
Amazonian, appeared to have been ſtole
from the ſtatue of the god of love.
With all this, ſhe had a great deal of
ſpirit and gaiety ; but as much caprice
in her humour, as there was oddneſs in
her figure.

We entered the garden like ſo many
mad people, ſinging, dancing, running
one after another, pulling the flowers,
and ſticking them in the head-dreſſes
and perriwigs.   The old *Marquiſs* was
one of the firſt at theſe gambols : in
paſſing by the ſtatues, I expected ſome
remarks conformable to the ſubject,
but

but *Madamoiselle* XII. and XIII. only gave a fide glance at them, and went on without fpeaking a fingle word. *Madamoiselle* XI. *faid*, here's good inftruction for the veftals. *Madamoiselle* X. *cried*, they don't think we know what they mean. The *Marquifs* would fain have engaged fome difcourfe on this head, but beginning to promote it, was bid to hold his tongue, for an old libertine: in a word, the ftatues loft their end ; and as I remembered the obfcenity of the firft company, and the aufterity of the fecond in the fame place, I was very well pleafed with the medium between both, obferved by our four nymphs.

WE advanced towards the grafs-plat, where the evennefs and verdure invited the ladies to dance regularly ; a minuet, admirably performed, terminated in a chorus of fongs, after which every one fat down at their eafe: the women placed themfelves on a bank at the foot of the ftatues, and we men threw ourfelves between thofe marble figures. They

They proposed some little plays, of
which they had a great number, and
the most part were very diverting and
ingenious. I remember in that of *Com-
parisons, Madamoiselle* X. whom I had
not suspected of any great share of
judgment, gave two replys which very
much pleased all the company. On the
question *to what do you compare my
thought?* She said, *To an egg.* Marriage being the thought, she was to
prove the comparison. *Nothing more
easy,* answered she, with her accustomed vivacity, *for neither are good after
the first day.* On another question, the
word being a *base-viol,* and the thought
a *pillow,* there was not one of us could
find a comparison, till she cried, *I have
it, both of them soften the disquiets of
the day.*

WE played also at *Proverbs,* at the
Alphabet of Love, at *good mother* An-
gotte; at, *Do you sell any ribond?*
and many others, for there was none
in the assembly that had not something
of this nature to propose. The forfeits

   were

were taken and redeemed with an infinity of pleaſantry, which continued
without any abatement, till ſupper-time,
when the ſteward approached with his
ordinary ſolemnity, and gravely told us,
the table attended us.   This man was
an old domeſtic, who had brought up
the *Chevalier*. The women took it
into their heads to make him break
through the formality of his pace, and
began with throwing herbs and flowers
at him, then pinched him, and whip-
ped him with their handkerchiefs ; we
joined them in this diverſion, and the
poor man took his flight; we purſued
him laughing quite into the houſe, where
we arrived all diſconcerted and out of
breath.

THE frolick however, had not taken away our appetites, we ſeated our-
ſelves with a very good will, on ſight
of diſhes, which were not leſs grateful
to the ſmell than taſte. We became
now, ſomewhat more ſerious, though
not more reſerved than we had been.
The women, treated each other with
                                        the

the title of *Madame*, inftead of *Madamoifelle*, which feeming a little ftrange
to me, I mentioned it to the gentleman
that fat next to me, who told me it was
their cuftom; moft of them, having
already had the honour of being mo-
thers, and all of them known to be in
the way of being fo.   They had alfo
a cuftom whenever they fpoke of the
young gentlemen, either of the court or
army, to omit calling them *Monfieur,* or
giving them any other title; and named
them familiarly *Damon, Eraftes,* &c.
to which they thought they had a right,
as having been their lovers, or might
become fo in a day or two.   But I obferved, that when on any occafion they
mentioned women of condition, they
treated them with no more refpect; frequently neglecting to fay *Madame,* and
contenting themfelves with calling them
plain *Belifa, Dorimena,* &c. but the fource
of this freedom, I never could find out.

As the appetite grew flack, the defire
of talking and laughing revived. Raillery was renewed, and a thoufand a-
greeable

greeable circumſtances brought upon
the carpet, which would loſe the greateſt
part of their beauty, by the repetition.
It is enough to ſay, that what could
ſupport converſation with the ſame life,
as when it begun, during a whole night,
muſt be very far from inſipid. Nor
could any thing groſs or ſhocking to the
underſtanding, give ſatisfaction for ſuch
a length of time; but, that which a-
muſed the mind, and diſſipated all ſorts
of cares and inquietudes, certainly deſerves the name of pleaſant. I know of
nothing more worthy of being called ſo,
than where, without the leaſt encroach-
ment on modeſty and innocence, the
two ſexes mutually do all they can, to
pleaſe each other. Virtue does not appear amiable, in a woman who is too
auſtere; and vice, when ſhewn in a
groſs light is deteſtable; but in an entertainment ſuch as this, where in the
midſt of all that could regale the ſenſes,
to have nothing eſcape, either of word
or geſture, contrary to decency and
good manners, yet the obſervance due
to both maintained without affectation
or conſtraint, was a conduct which I
                                    never

never think on without applause. Play-
ing upon words, sportive jests, pleasant
stories, humourous adventures, intrigues
of the theatre, were the subjects of our
discourse : but I could perceive no sha-
dow of malice for the reputation of o-
thers, no envy of merit, no jealousy of
partiality, no ambition of preference,
nor was even any thing of that vanity,
which I had imagined inherent to women of their character, to be found a-
mong them. Each seemed to impute her
good fortune in pleasing, rather to the
caprice of her lover, than her own merit. They seemed to know the temper
of mankind so well, as to be sensible,
that oftentimes those women, who had
in reality the least attractions, were liked
best ; and none were uneasy at seeing
the choice made of another, because
every one hoped to triumph in her
turn, and charm even the man who had
most neglected her. In fine, I perceived
they had not only customs and manners,
but also principles, such as could alone
render their way of life satisfactory to
themselves, and agreeable to others ;
and this œconomy, if I may so call it,

of

of mind and behaviour, made me feveral times fay to the old *Marquifs*,
that I thought them charming creatures.

IT was impoffible to grow tired and
heavy in an affembly, where one pleafure was inftantly fucceeded by another,
and frefh fubjects of entertainment were
continually arifing. When difcourfe
was at an ebb, finging fupplied the va-
cancy. *Madamoifelle* X. and XI. gave
us a great many fongs, which after having heard fucceffively, we teftified our
applaufe by clapping our hands, as at the
opera ; they then proceeded to couplets,
and ftanza's of four lines, the others
joining in the chorus ; and this brought
us far into the night, when the *Chevalier* willing that *Madamoifelle* XII.
fhould alfo difplay her talent, propofed
a dance, but fhe obferving the moon
fhone very bright, and caft a delightful luftre on the trees, told him, fhe
rather wifhed to pafs the remainder of
the time in the garden. We comply-
ed with her requeft, finding, indeed,
that after fitting four hours at the table,
the

the freſhneſs of the air very reviving.
We walked ſeveral turns, after which
ſat down on that beautiful graſs-plat,
where we had paſſed ſo much time before ſupper. The *Marquiſs*, who con-
dućted us thither, had a deſign in it;
he wanted ſome ſuch little ſtories of their
lives, as thoſe ladies had given us at our
ſecond feaſt, and had no ſooner commu-
nicated his requeſt, than our four women cried out at once, they were ready
to oblige him, and *Madamoiſelle* X. immediately began.

My life, *ſaid ſhe, with the utmoſt
gaiety*, has nothing in it more heroic
than my adventures on the theatre:
but I have had the honour of making
a conqueſt over a hero, of whom I can
relate to you ſomething pretty ſingular.
He had heard of me in the fartheſt
part of the north, for what place ſo
diſtant, that my chains have not been
carried?   Having been dangerouſly
wounded in a battle, he made a pretence that his cure not being fully per-
fećted, he muſt côme to conſult the
ſurgeons at *Paris*; but his principal
                                motive

motive was to see me, at least he told me so on his first arrival; but I afterwards found he had, in effect, reason to take care of his wounds, the ill cure of which had left somewhat behind that threatened his life. I was not insensible of the passion he had for me; but being engaged at that time with another lover, who adored me with an equal tenderness, and whom I did not chuse to abandon, I set myself to contrive some way to carry on a double intrigue, and at last hit upon one which answered all my hopes. I went to the surgeons, who had my stranger under their care, and making no scruple of acquainting them with the designs he had upon me, entreated they would tell me sincerely, if his condition would permit him to gratify his inclination without prejudice to his health. On which they frankly replied, that being much worse than he imagined himself, his life would be in the utmost danger, if the dictates of his passion prevailed.

THIS answer was perfectly agreeable to my wish; I then told them, it depended

ed on them to do me an extraordinary
service, secure their patient from the
misfortune he was going to bring upon
himself, and also oblige another worthy
person. A small present rendered them
at my devotion, and I then desired them
to give me a formal certificate of their
decision, and to acquaint the stranger
with the true state of his case, and deter
him from prosecuting his amorous intentions. They consented, and I left
them very well satisfied with the success
of my visit. I then acquainted my lover with the occasion that presented me
considerable advantages, without any
injury to him, and shewed him the certificate of the truth of what I said. The
doubts he was in, made him at first re-
reproach me; but I soon silenced him,
by saying, he ought rather to applaud
this testimony of my fidelity; for if I
had a mind to deceive him, I could have
found artifices sufficient for that purpose,
or might have quitted him absolutely,
since it was not in his power to preserve
my favours without my inclination.
This last argument had the desired effect, if he was not convinced of my in-
integrity,

tegrity, he loved me too well not to pretend he was fo, and permitted me to act in this matter as I found moft to my advantage.

HAVING thus gained my point with him, my next bufinefs was to manage my ftranger; I told him, that nothing but the dread of reproaching myfelf, as the caufe of his death, fhould make me refufe all the proofs he wifhed of my affection; and as I was poffeffed of the fincereft gratitude, refpect, and love for him, I was willing to fulfil all the duties of a miftrefs, excepting thofe which I was convinced muft be fatal to him: the injunction that had been laid on him by his furgeons, made him readily acquiefce to what I faid, and he thought himfelf happy, that a woman, fuch as I, would confent to pafs the days with him, and deny herfelf all other entertainments for a lover who was incapable of receiving her in the nights. We prefently agreed for a large fum, which was to be paid monthly to me; and I thought myfelf the moft fortunate creature in the world, rolling in money by
the

the liberality of two lovers, and perfectly tranquil in my mind, by having
nothing to accuse myself with. The
lover of the day sent his coach to bring
me to him every morning, and treated
me with that can be called delicious till
the evening, and the other waited e-
very night to receive, and carress me
till the break of day. This agreeable
life lasted six weeks; never should I
have been weary of it, but, alass! on
what slight accidents our happiness
sometimes depends !   When I thought
my fortune established, a cursed footman———.

'TILL this instant *Madamoiselle* X.
had gone on very seriously with her narrative, but here a fit of laughing had
seized her with such force, that none
but those who were present, can be capable of conceiving it. All our desires
that she would proceed in her history,
were of no effect to moderate this transport, and as she was obliged to hold her
sides, we also could not forbear laughing to keep her company ; at last,——
Oh ! that cursed footman, *resumed she*,
he

he muſt be a *Muſcovite*, for I am told
thoſe ſavage people know nothing of
gallantry : this curſed fellow I ſay, conducting me home one evening to the very
door of my chamber, with an offici-
ouſneſs that I did not deſire from him,
perceived my lover, who attended me,
and had undreſſed himſelf, and put on
a night-gown. Four minutes after this
I heard a loud knocking at the door, and
immediately entered my lover of the
day, having, no doubt, been informed
by that deviliſh wretch, of what he had
ſeen—.

HERE ſhe fell into a ſecond fit of
laughter, which almoſt took away her
breath. We affected to be very grave,
and the *Marquiſs* cried, I ſee nothing
to laugh at in all this. It was in vain,
we could not ſtop her laughter ; and it
was with much difficulty ſhe brought
out, I laugh at the remembrance of it,
ſaid ſhe ; never was there ſo pleaſant a
ſcene : the poor gentleman was in his
cap and night-gown, covered with plaiſ-
ters and cataplaſms : judge of the perplexity I was in between two men who
liked

liked so ill to see each other. The laugh
renewing again, put a stop to her discourse ; but she recovered herself by
degrees, and promised to give us the
remainder of this detail. I had nevertheless, *continued she*, presence enough
of mind to ask him what he wanted
with me so late ? To which he replied,
he knew no terms capable of reproaching my perfidiousness as it deserved. I
was very much affronted at these words ;
but reflecting, that in strict justice he
might be shocked at my conduct, I attempted to turn the whole adventure into a matter of pleasantry. This affair,
*said I, with all the gaiety I could as-
sume*, may be judged two ways ; either by *example*, or by *right*. If we
go by the former, here is a gallant man,
continued I, pointing to my lover, who
contents himself with seeing me about
twelve hours in the four and twenty,
though he does not pay less for my company than you do. In *France*, example
is a rule. However, *added I*, if you
do not approve of our ways, and imagined you had me solely, during these
six weeks, and pretend that you paid
me

me for four and twenty hours each day, it only remains to refund half of the sum I have received.

WHILE I was speaking, he had time to make his reflections, or perhaps the resolution of my lover, who did not appear the least astonished at his presence, I know not which, but he went directly away, without giving any answer to what I said. I longed impatiently for the morning, however, in suspence whether his coach would come for me as usual or not, and instead of it, received a letter with an hundred *Louis-d'ors* enclosed. He made me no reproaches, but acknowledged, that in his situation, he ought not to have expected a woman, like me, should sacrifice her pleasures: he thank'd me for the complaisance I shewed him, and had sent me the last token of his gratitude. I could not but confess there was something noble and generous in this proceeding ; if I had resented it, I should have sent him back his hundred *Louis-d'ors* ; but I am good natured ; I forgave the little vexation he had given me, me, and did him the pleasure to accept his money.

THERE was somewhat in this recital, full of true humour and agreeable to the character of the person who made it.---*Madamoiselle* XI. having had time to prepare what she had to say, begun in the following manner.

I have had lovers, *said she*, as who has not you will think? but what may perhaps surprize you a little at first hearing; I have had forty, neither more nor less; for I have always taken care to keep an exact account: if you ask how this happened, I should be in some perplexity my self how to answer; but some I quitted, and others quitted me. Fops that were not capable of an attachment above the space of fifteen days; —officers who staid in *Paris* but a few weeks; --men of the long robe, or of the church, who feared scandal at three or four months end :----one is not mistress of the constancy of others; but I protest to you, that I never had two intrigues at a time; so that all my infi-

C   delities

delities are oweing to the men. It is now
some years since an honest rich *Financier*, took a great liking to my person: I was then at liberty, and gave no
rebuff to his passion. We were just on
the point of coming to an agreement,
when my cabinet happening to be open,
he saw a paper entitled, a list of my lovers. There they all were set down,
indeed, names and titles, with the date
of my engagement with each, and se-
paration.

I perceived the effect this discovery
had on him : a cold poison could not
have operated more powerfully : for my
part, I was not disconcerted in the least,
and knowing he was a man of good
sense, I attempted to convince him by
reason, that I had not been to blame.
Do you not know any woman, *said I*,
that has been married ten years ? Yes,
answered he. I will suppose her amiable, *rejoined I*, and if so, and she
should become a widow, would you
have a disgust for her, because she had
been for ten years the wife of another ?
No, *said he*. Well then, *replied I*, I
have

have lived a life of gallantry, and have had no greater a number of nights in ten years, than she who has been married for that time has enjoyed, and never have had more than one engagement at a time : Where then is the difference of having been possessed by forty, or one man ? This argument had weight with my *Financier*, and all was concluded to our mutual satisfaction.

WE agreed with *Madamoiselle* XI. that in effect it is much the same between a woman who had passed ten years with one man, and her who had forty successively in the same space. But, *said one of the company*, must not such a multitude of engagements occasion a strange disorder in the heart ? No, *replied she*, it rather renders us more amiable : in what consists the merit of a woman, if it is not in an agreeableness of manners and mind ? And what can give us that but experience, which is not to be acquired without exercise and variety ? Your chaste widow has but one mode of

pleasing,

pleafing, which happened to be the tafte of him who was her hufband : now we have a thoufand arts of charming, and whoever makes an effay, and pays us well, will find a girl from the *Opera* is a treafure.

THOUGH none of us offered to make this effay, yet we acknowledged the juftice of what fhe faid, and that nothing could be more feducing than herfelf and her companions. Even myfelf, who judged of things by a different principle than this affembly, ceafed to wonder fuch women made fo ftrong an impreffion on an infinite number of men, who fet nothing in competition with pleafure.

Madamoifelle XII. was fomewhat lefs ready than the two former, to begin her narrative. In fpeaking of herfelf, fhe confulted lefs to amufe us, than to magnify the power of her own charms; after a paufe; however, fhe obliged us as the two former. It will be difficult for me, *faid fhe*, to make you comprehend in what a perplexity my laft engagement

gagement involved me. I was follicited by two men, between whom I
was a long time before I could determine. The *D.* of * * *, and *L* * *,
equally paid their adorations; but it was
to the laft I gave the preference. Not
but I know very well how to put a due
difference between a nobleman, and a
man of bufinefs. It is highly pleafing
whenever one appears in any public
walks, or at the *Opera*, or other fhews,
to hear people cry, *who is fhe?* and the
anfwer, *a celebrated beauty, miftrefs of
the D. of * * *;* to which, perhaps a-
nother joins, *he loves her to madnefs, he
ruins himfelf for her.* This fpreads ones
fame, and procures one refpect from all
who we have any dealings with; but
as I do not go much abroad, I thought
I had little reafon to regard what was
faid of me without doors, and had no
occafion to be obliged to the quality of
my lover, for being obeyed and well
ufed at home by thofe I pay. Befides,
I confidered that men of quality put
their miftreffes into a continual hurry;
they are fond of having their amours
public, they bring their friends to fup-

per, they lose all respect for the woman
they keep, and on some occasions are
apt to treat her as they would do a girl
of the town.   In fine, *L* * * was my
choice; he is rich, luxurious, generous
and constant: there were two motives
which inclined me in his favour: the
D. offered me fifty *Louis-d'ors* for my
company a few hours; this compliment shewed, that whatever love he
had for me, he had very little esteem,
and made me reply to him, Fye, my
lord *D. said I,* you will give me fifty *Louis-d'ors* to night, and leave me
the most miserable woman in the world
to-morrow.

He afterwards endeavoured to re-
trieve my good graces, by proposing a
pension for four years, and an assu-
rance of continuing it for life, if at
the end of that time we approved of
prolonging our correspondence: but I
had too much spirit to forgive his former offer so soon; and two days after
an accident happened, which determined me to give over all thoughts of
him for ever.

The

THE D------ſs *** his wife, having heard of his frequent viſits to me, eaſily gueſſed the occaſion ; and either through love and jealouſy of his perſon, or fear of the expences which ſhe might well think would attend a converſation with me, became exceſſively diſquieted. I never gave myſelf the trouble to examine into the motives of her behaviour; it was ſufficient for me to know I was affronted.

ONE day I was prevailed upon by two of the *D*------'s friends, who uſed ſometimes to accompany him in the viſits he made me, to go with them to the ſtar. We had not been long in the walks, before we ſaw two ladies, who having left their coach upon the hill, came toward us on foot, and I perceived had their eyes very earneſtly fixed upon me. The gentlemen ſaluting them with a ſignificant ſmile, made me preſently apprehend what afterwards enſued, and my ſuſpicions were confirmed, when caſting my eyes toward the hill, I ſaw the *D*------'s

C 4   coach,

coach, and the livery of madame the
D----fs, but if I had been lefs penetrating, they took care not to leave me long
in doubt.   It muft be confeft, *faid the*
D-----fs, in a low voice to the other lady,
that the creature is handfome enough.--
I did not think fhe had been fo agreeable ; it is pity, *continued fhe, much*
louder than before, that fome one does
not inform her, that if fhe perfifts in
receiving the carreffes of my hufband,
fhe will be in an hofpital within thefe
four days. This menace which I heard
very diftinctly, put me into the utmoft
rage, and I could not forbear anfwering;
go madame, *faid I,* it is not my fault if
I am more lovely than your grace, and
I think it beneath a woman of your quality to take notice of me.---Look well
after your *D * * *,* there is no body defigns to deprive you of him, and I fhould
be forry to have it faid, I made the
D-------fs of *D * * ** die with jealoufy.
She paffed on with a difdainful air,
without feeming to give any attention to
what I faid ; and though I was glad I
had returned her infult, yet was I fo
much piqued at, that I could fcarce re-
                                    frain

frain burfting into tears. I was refolute to return to the city, and affoon as I arrived, told the two friends of the *D****, that I faw into the trick they had played me, but that it fhould be the laft, either of him or them. I gave orders at my door, which nothing was capable of making me retract; and the fame day accepted the offers of *Z****, with whom I have ever fince continued in a very happy fituation. He has no other fault but loving me too well, however, as I do not hate him, I can forgive even his jealoufies, and have fo much complaifance, as to give my company to no other perfon.----This is the firft time I have taken the opportunity of his abfence to fup with thefe gentlemen, the greateft part of whom are my old friends; and though I think it ridiculous to have bound myfelf by oaths, yet I do not repent of having made them, or have ever been tempted to break them.

THE recital of *Madamoifelle* XII. very much engroffed my attention, not for the reafons fhe imagined, that is to fay, on the account of her beauty, or

C 5   the

the *D*----'s paſſion; but I was ſtruck
with her language; her principles: and a-
bove all, that native ſincerity which only
ſerved to make others laugh. I remembered what the *Marquiſs* had told me of this
third ſupper, where he had promiſed
I ſhould find nothing reſembling the
two former: I found in effect ſomething
agreeable ſingular in the two women
of the *Opera*, but yet more in the character of *Madamoiſelle* XII. which was
altogether new to me. It ſhewed me
that a medium between modeſty, and
debauch which before I had believed
impoſſible, and I could not help admiring a woman who without knowing virtue, had the image of it in her
mind, and ſeemed even ſcrupeouſly attached to it. As I now perceived there
were a number of ſuch ſort of women
in *Paris*, and equally experienced the
pleaſures of their converſation. I did
not wonder that many men employed
the ſuperfluity of their wealth in entertaining them; but though I regarded
this as a piece of luxury unknown to
our anceſtors, I confeſſed that ſetting
aſide religion, which admits no medium

um between vice and virtue, there were few civil rights to oppofe it. I found alfo that they held a diftinguifhed rank among the pleafures, and in fuppofing that all the women of this clafs main- tained the fame referve which I now faw before my eyes, with the fame liberty and the fame charms, allowed there was nothing in their converfation offenfive to decency and good manners, but on the contrary perfectly agreeable to both.

WHILE I was taken up with this thought, they had engaged *Madamoi- felle* XIII. to give us her ftory. I am the moft whimfical creature in life, *faid fhe, with the moft charming tone*; I ne- ver could join four phrafes together, and yet you oblige me to make a long dif- courfe.----My talent is all for exclama- tion ; however, if you have patience to hear to the end, you may perhaps com- prehend what I would fay. I remem- ber that about thirty years ago.----The mad creature ! *cried the Chevalier in- terrupting her*, fhe is not above eight- teen.----See now, *refumed fhe*, you for- get that you are to liften till I have done,

but you will have more cauſe to obſerve
me better. It is of my mother I am
ſpeaking ; it is about thirty years as I
was ſaying, and I remember becauſe
ſhe was always repeating it to me, that
being married into a diſtant province,
ſhe wrote to her brother, who was *valet de chambre* to a young lord at *Paris*,
that ſhe had, had a very extraordinary
dream.----O ! theſe dreams, I have had
ſome that have been very odd, but I
ſpeak of that of my mother.------She
dreamt, though ſhe had never had any
children, that ſhe was the mother of a
daughter extremely beautiful, who had
raiſed the fortune of the whole family.
Her brother whom I ſcarce dare call my
uncle, becauſe he is at preſent in the en-
joyment of a very great poſt ; anſwered, that ſhe ought not to neglect the
premonitions of heaven : that if ſhe
ſhould have a daughter, it was her duty to bring her up with the utmoſt care,
and ſend her young to *Paris*, in order
to be better accompliſhed, and her natural talents being improved, ſhe might
be put into ſome way of fullfilling the
prediction. Twelve whole years after
this

this dream paſſed over without my mother proving pregnant, and ſhe was beginning to loſe all hopes, when in the thirteenth I came into the world.----A rare piece, tis certain ; nature doubtleſs made many efforts before ſhe brought this workmanſhip to perfection.----All her expectations now revived : ſhe found me handſome, that is to ſay, well enough, ſuch as you ſee me. She educated me very well for a girl of my condition ; and when I was twelve years of age, it came into her head to take what meaſures ſhe could for verifying her dream. Accordingly ſhe wrote to my uncle who ſtill continued with his lord, acquainting him that I was of an age proper to be put to ſomething ; that he would be agreeably ſurprized to find me ſo beautiful, that ſhe would ſend me in the ſtage coach, which would bring me to him in ſix days.---- That it was on him ſhe depended for getting me inſtructed in ſuch things as the country could not beſtow on me, and afterwards to put me prentice to ſome gainful and genteel buſineſs, deſiring him above all things, to watch the

coming

coming in of the coach. This letter was sent to *Paris* by the post, but my uncle happening to be abroad, when it arrived, the porter laid it on a table in the anti-chamber of the palace till his return. The lord seeing it, thought he had a right to examine the contents, which finding so much in favour of a young girl, a sudden inclination came into his thoughts. He was then far advanced in years, but his taste for pleasure far from being diminished. He locked up the letter carefully, and when my uncle came back, told him somewhat of importance had happened, bad him take a horse that moment, and carry a letter from him to a certain nobleman, then at *Versailles*, who, he said, would give him farther orders.

My uncle transported with the confidence his lord reposed in him, in a matter which seemed of so much moment, departed on the instant. The letter contained a request to the nobleman to shut up the messenger for four whole days under lock and key, and not suffer him to return till the expiration

ration of that time, whatever he should
alledge. In a word, this desire was
punctually complied with, my uncle
was conducted into a chamber by himself, where they told him, that for some
secret reasons which ought not however to give him any alarm, he must be
content to remain four days. It was
two before the coach was expected,
and the lord employed that time in
causing an apartment to be furnished in
a street some distance from his palace,
and placing a servant-maid in it, telling
her, he would bring her a very beautiful mistress; then dressing himself in a
habit suitable to his design, he came to
receive me in the coach. On his asking for his neice, I threw myself upon
his neck, and calling him my dear uncle, embraced him for my father, my
mother and myself. He put me immediately into a hackney-coach, and
conducted me to the lodging he had
prepared for me. He promised to make
me as happy as a little queen. Nothing
in effect was wanting to charm the senses of a young girl, rich cloaths, delicate food, fine wines, and a servant who
thought

thought herſelf happy in obeying me.
In fine, he told me, that *Paris* being a
dangerous place, he did not think proper to leave me all night expoſed to
evil ſpirits and robbers: thus I found
a moſt paſſionate lover, inſtead of an
uncle. You will aſk, perhaps, if I was
abſolutely deceived, or did not willingly ſuffer myſelf to yield to the en-
chantments of pleaſure, and I am too
ſincere to diſguiſe the matter. The
charms of courtſhip, the ſight of a thouſand pretty toys, and the hopes of living at eaſe blinded me. My uncle returned two days after. I don't know
in what manner his lord diſcovered to
him his artifice, but he conſented to
ſay nothing of it, and the reward of
his complaiſance was a conſiderable employment my noble lover procured for
him. My mother, to whom I gave
an account of what happened, both in
regard of myſelf and uncle, wrote to
me, that my father being dead, ſhe
would diſpoſe of what he had left her
in poſſeſſion of, and come to *Paris*,
and ſettle with me, which ſhe ſoon after did, and we lived in this manner
till

till the death of my lover, who be-
queathed me a penfion for life of twelve
hundred livres, which would have been
fufficient to have put me in fome handfome bufinefs, if my uncle had vouch-
fafed to have taken any care of my ef-
tablifhment, but having attained an honourable ftation himfelf, he refufed to
fee me after the death of his lord. The
grief of finding myfelf abandoned. A
long habitude of eafe, and the perfuafions of my mother, who liked to live
in opulence, prevailed on me to liften
to the offers of a gentleman of the long
robe, with whom I at prefent am. He
is rich, and good-natured; his frequent
fits of the gout, allow me a great deal
of liberty, which I never abufe. But
mercy on us! *cried fhe*, I believe you
are all half a fleep, for I find myfelf at
the end of my hiftory, in a languor
which is little better.

We all affured her, that on the contrary, fhe had very much amufed us.
I indeed had been more fo than any
one elfe by fome ideas which her difcourfe had occafioned. The manner
in

in which she had been seduced, served
as an explication of many others who I
had seen quite abandoned, yet who once
were innocent, and convinced me that
what dissolution soever we meet with
in a sex, whose peculiar characteristic is
bashfulness and modesty, it is primarily
owing to the artifices of men. Too
ready indeed they are when once viola-
ted to stop at nothing, and from the pu-
rest part of the creation degenerate into
the most corrupt.---She therefore who
sees her error, and reclaims after being
once a victim, deserves more praise,
than the ill-judging world is willing to
allow. Others again, who may pursue
the same path of pleasure, yet looks
with horror on the yet deeper abyss of
guilt and shame, in which the most de-
praved part of the sex are fallen, have
some degree of merit. Some remains
of good sentiments, after the wreck of
their virtue are still to be found in them,
and it was in this last rank I placed those
I was now among.

AURORA now beginning to pro-
claim the approach of day, our ladies
thought

thought it time to take their leaves, but before they did so, had the courage to enter the lists with the nightingales, who were tuning their melodious notes among the trees, and did not cease on the more loud and striking airs which issued from the womens throats, and in which we men also sometimes joined in chorus.---Our mutual vivacity carrying us into somewhat more into confusion, than had hitherto been. Fye, *cried Madamoiselle* XI. what *Persiflage!* this word being altogether new to me, or rather having heard it several times, without being able to comprehend the meaning; I asked the old *Marquiss*, by my troth *answered he*, I use it myself very often, yet know it no better than you, but I believe it signifies what we have been doing all this night; and that is just nothing at all. This occasioned our demanding the explanation of *Madamoiselle* XI. from whom we had heard it; but she protested she could give no other account of it, than that she had heard it a thousand times applied on such occasions as the present. All the company made the same confession of
their

their ignorance, and of a hundred perfons whom I have fince confulted, I never found one capable of giving me the
definition I defired. At laft, to join
grammar with my hiftory, I have found
out myfelf, that *Perfiflage* is the art of
raillying agreeably by reafons and figures
of fpeech, which the perfon to whom
it is ufed, either does not underftand, or
takes in a wrong fenfe; but our ladies,
and indeed many others, from whom
more might be expected, did not think
themfelves obliged to know what they
faid, provided they faid it with a good
grace. Our entertainment concluded
with a grand dance, to fhew us that they
yielded not to droufinefs, but as the fun
appeared, they retired like the ftars: each
threw herfelf into the coach which
waited to conduct them home, and took
leave with the fame gaiety as they had
entered.

As I had heard no mention of any
gratuity, I asked the *Marquifs* if fome
Lewis d'ors were not expected from
me.---No, no, *anfwered he*, thefe are
women who are above payment, they
come

come readily to a private supper, and to receive pleasure themselves, as well as give it. I do not tell you, but if you find them amiable enough to desire to see them again, they will refuse a diamond, a watch, or some such toy; but then the present must be accompanied with gallantry and respect: I thanked him for this instruction, and found the women so agreeable, that I told him I would not wish it to be the last time of meeting, and that I should like to give a supper once or twice a month, as I went to the *Opera* once or twice a week.

NOTWITHSTANDING the pleasures of this night, the whole next day taken up in sleep, did not seem too long to repair the waste of so many waking hours. But the succeeding one I began to think of paying my compliments to Monsieur and Madame *de B* * * *, I went to their house, and the reproaches of Monsieur for an absence which seemed to him too long, persuaded me that he took a real satisfaction in seeing me.

I

I could not however affure myfelf, that madame had the fame fentiments: politenefs and fweetnefs, were the infeparable companions of all her words and actions; but then, a fevere and awful modefty fhone through every thing fhe faid and did, and kept me from flattering myfelf too far. The fame behaviour in any other woman, might have been taken for conftraint; but in her, it was too eafy not to be the effect of nature. It was in the afternoon, that I made my vifit, and *Monfieur de B * * ** entreated me in the moft friendly and familiar terms, to ftay and fup with his wife by his bed-fide, but fhe prevented my anfwering, by faying, I fear, my dear, you intrude too far on monfieur the *Count*'s good nature; do you not think he has already a party made, where he will find more amufement than in fupping alone with us? to which I replied, that without doubt, there were twenty places where I might go, but as I had no formal engagement for that evening, I would willingly accept the offer of monfieur *de B * * **, if fhe had the goodnefs to confent. In fine,

fine, I ſtayed, and all the pleaſures in
the world, never came up to this agreeable ſupper. I eat little, though the
table was elegantly furniſhed; but I
found in the charms of madame *de*
B * * *, the moſt delicious regale for all
my ſenſes. The table was placed within two foot of the bed, I ſat juſt oppoſite to her, and had opportunity to
obſerve her more than ever I had done
before. What new perfections did I
now diſcover! what rich treaſures of
beauty, wit, and graces! with the admiration which ſhe inſpired in me,
there entered alſo ſome ſparks of fire,
which then kindled in my heart, and
never ſince has ceaſed to burn; but,
with ſo much liberty of ſeeing and
hearing her, I thought ſhe could not
have appeared leſs charming to all mankind; and, it was the belief, that I rendered her no more than juſtice which
kept me yet, from diſtinguiſhing the
true nature of my ſentiments.

I went home ſo full of her, that the
reaſons, which before had determined
me, to put ſome diſtance between my
visits,

vifits, became every moment more
weak. The next day, I longed impatiently for the evening, and went
again at the fame hour. She feemed a little furprized at feeing me,
but it lafted not a moment; her hufband teftified all the joy, that he was
capable of feeling in his fituation; we
entered into a converfation, in which
he appeared no lefs fatisfied than myfelf: I was about to retire, when
looking on me with the moft obliging
fmile, can you forgive me, *faid he*, if
I afk where you are engaged to night?
no where, *replied I*, any more than
yefterday. Why then will you not
ftay with us, *refumed he*, at leaft, if
you have not already had too much
of indifferent eating, and worfe company? I durft not make any reply, till
I had confulted the looks of madame
de B * * *; her eyes were caft down,
but I imagined, I found nothing in
them to oppofe my defires. I am fo
far, *anfwered I*, from having had too
much of either, that I fhall gladly accept the offer of more. I am of a humour, *added I*, different from moft of
those

thofe of my age; it does not incline
me to thofe noify pleafures, to which
youth is ordinarily addicted; and I find
more felicity where there is a maturity
of judgment, provided it be accompanied
with good nature, both which I have
experienced here. It will be very happy for me, *replied he*, if you believe
me capable of difcovering thofe two
good qualities in you; but I fhall perceive your fentiments of us, by the fatisfaction you fhall take in feeing us, and
that fatisfaction alfo, by the frequency of
your vifits.

c repeat here the invitations of monfieur *de* B * * *, to juftify in fome mea-
fure, the affiduity with which I continued to vifit him, and to fup almoft
every night at his houfe. I am very
far from pretending, that the affection
he feemed to have for me, was the fole
motive, yet it ferved at that time to
difguife from myfelf, the true fentiments
of my heart, which became more ftrong
by this delufion, as it prevented me
from making any efforts to oppofe
them. I ought never to mention the
D word

word *Love*, without horror, becauſe
that fatal paſſion has plung'd me into
misfortunes, which can have no period
but with my life; but then, it has alſo
left ſome charming impreſſions, which
takes from me the power of even re-
penting having been the victim of it.

THE ſight of madame *de B* * * * ſo
often, the opportunities I had of diſ-
covering more and more of her wit,
her virtue and her goodneſs was like a
fatal drug, which made drunk my reaſon. It was not an exceſs of pleaſure,
no wild hurrying emotions, but a ſoft
delight, a ſweet habitude of mind
which I felt at firſt in the freedom of
her converſation; but too ſoon, I found
a dreadful change, inſtead of that tranquility, with which I had approached
her, that vivacity with which her preſence inſpired me,---of that gaiety with
which her diſcourſes animated me, I
fell into a condition which I cannot remember without aſtoniſhment: I deſired to ſee her with the utmoſt impatience, yet rejoiced not when I came
before her; but on the contrary, the
deepeſt

deepest shades of sorrow seemed to o-
vercast my spirits. I listened eagerly
whenever she spoke, but scarce had the
power of answering:--- that face, which
I had now gazed upon with admiration
and complaisance, now rendered my
eyes immoveable, and fixed in a kind
of stupid languor, which, as often as I
have surprized myself in, threw me into confusion. A sudden glance, like
that of lightning, would sometimes
rouse me from my lethargy, but all that
mingled sweetness and vivacity with
which her every look was accompanied,
had not power to draw from me any
more than a half smile, which ended
before it was well begun. Thus did I
suffer, without knowing the cause of
my suffering. I was disquieted, yet
had no subject of disquiet. I sighed
yet had nothing to fear, nor nothing to
regret. Monsieur *de B* * * *, perceive-
ing the change in my humour, often
asked me with a friendly anxiety, if
any thing had happen to afflict me? to
which I answered, with a great deal of
sincerity, that I was ignorant myself,
from whence proceeded this alteration,

but

but confeffed I found a confiderable one,
and imagined fome diftemper was grow-
ing on me.   His wife did not afk me
the fame queftions, but I thought I obferved in her eyes, fomewhat that de-
noted an intereft in my melancholly.
Her leaft attention was pernicious to
my peace ;---my fenfes were in confufion
at every word fhe fpoke, whatever fhe
touched had a kind of magic, an invincible attraction in it, which permitted
none of my faculties to retain the force
of operating.

THERE now wanted no farther proofs
to inform me of the truth, of my unhappy fituation.   The misfortune was
not arrived to this extremity, without
my being fadly convinced of the weaknefs of my heart; yet defended as I
thought myfelf, by my principles, I
thought I might indulge an inclination
which had no aim, but what was con-
fiftant with innocence and virtue.---Ig-
norant of the delufions of pleafure, it
grew upon me by imperceptible degrees; yet I muft do this juftice to the
force of my refolution, that it was not
through

through any fear of not having a sufficient command over myself, that I took
the measures I soon after did : but because finding a visible decay in myself
through want of sleep and appetite, I
attempted to wean my heart from a pleasure, which threatned me with the loss
of my reason, or my life.---What *said
I*, is there any inclination so sweet any
illusion so flattering ; any charm so powerful to make me entertain, even the
most distant wish of violating the laws
of hospitality and marriage.---No---all
amiable as madame *de B* * * * undoubt-
edly is, I will renounce the heaven her
conversation bestows, and condemn my
self to everlasting banishment, since I
cannot continue to see her, without danger of breaking through those rules I
have prescribed myself.

In this determination, I went one
day to monsieur and madame *de B****,
and told them that being threatned with
the return of an ancient infirmity, I
should be obliged to confine myself to
my chamber, and observe a certain regimen, which would deprive me of the

honour

honour of feeing them for fome time. Monfieur *de B * * **, feemed extremely concerned, but having nothing to op- pofe againft the care of my health, contented himfelf with praying for my re-eftablifhment. Madame *de B* * **, of whom alfo I took leave, made me an anfwer in much the fame terms with her hufband, but not daring to truft my- felf too far, I did not examine her looks, left I fhould find fomething, which might have taken from me the power of purfuing my intentions: but when may we hope to fee you again, *faid Monfieur?* when he perceived me going, I know not, *anfwered I with a deep figh, which all my efforts were not able to reftrain*, but I hid my eyes from cafting them even once, on the face of his too lovely wife.

THE conflict within me at doing this, had been fo violent, that as I paffed the anti-chamber, fome tears, in fpite of me ran down my cheeks; I preferv- ed my conftancy, however, unfhaken, and went home, where I fhut myfelf up the remainder of the day; I paft
th-

the night in agonies inexpreſſible, nor did
the next morning, nor many enſuing
days, yield me any more tranquility.
Three whole weeks did I employ in
combating the emotions of my heart,
and repelling, as the moſt deadly poiſon, thoſe charming images which had
ſo lately made all my happineſs ; but
my reaſon at length convinced me, that
it was not from ſolitude I muſt expect
relief, and if I ſucceeded in the attempt
of loſing remembrance of that pleaſure,
and that pain I had experienced to ſo
violent an exceſs, it muſt be in noiſe,
hurry, and a multiplicity of amuſe-
ments.

DURING the time I was poſſeſſed of
thoſe tyrannic ſentiments, I had not the
power of going to any diverſion. Several private ſuppers had been propoſed
to me, all which I refuſed. *The Preſident,* monſieur *de la* * * *, and ſome
few other perſons, whom good manners
obliged me to viſit, were all I ſaw ; but
I now found it was time to take other
meaſures for my cure, which I accordingly did.

I went to dine at the Palace of * * *, a houfe celebrated for the numerous and polite affembly which always met there; but three or four hours which I paffed with them, feemed tedious to me: I found, as I had done feveral times before, that thefe mixed companies afforded nothing to attach either the mind or fenfes; but I had hoped, that the fight of new faces, new fafhions, and the pompous trifles which I could not fail of being entertained with, would make me lofe thofe ferious reflections which occafioned me fo much pain.

FROM thence I adjourned to the Playhoufe, where I imagined fo vaft a variety of objects might afford fome relaxation. As the fpectators, the mufic, the comedy itfelf, the liberty of going behind the fcenes, and talking to the actors, had heretofore paffed away fome idle hours. I had no fooner fet my foot in the pit, than I perceived the old *Marquifs* ftanding in a corner, fo bufy in examining the boxes and balconies, that I faluted him three times before

fore I could draw him out of his meditation; at laſt, turning toward me with
a great deal of warmth, have you ſeen
her? *cried he*, pointing to *madamoiſelle*
XIII. *the miſtreſs of the gentleman of
the long robe, one of thoſe that ſupped with
us.* She appeared indeed very ſparkling
as ſhe ſat in the balcony. It would be
glorious, *added he*, if we could get her
to night from her lover, who I hear is
got well of the gout.

I heard him without making any reply: he continued to preſs me to be
one of the party, to which I neither
yielded, nor abſolutely refuſed, and only told him, that I thought him very
happy in a temper which never altered
his reliſh for pleaſure, and then ſat down
to give attention, if it were poſſible for
me, to the repreſentation which juſt
then began.

WHILE I was endeavouring to liſten
to the comedy, the *Marquiſs* went up
to the balcony, and made uſe of all
his eloquence to tempt *Madamoiſelle*
XIII. by his offers, ſhe had perceived
him

him fpeaking to me, and her caprice,
it feems, having made her take fome
liking to me, fhe accepted his propofal
of a fupper, on two conditions, firft,
that he would engage me to be there,
and fecondly, that her lover, who was
to come at the end of the play, fhould
alfo be invited, becaufe, as fhe faid, it
would not be proper for her to quit
him, when he came on purpofe to attend her home; and befides, fhe had
reafons to wifh he might make an acquaintance with me. The *Marquifs*
conceived all that was favourable for
me in this explanation, and paffed over
the repugnance he had to having her
lover of the party. He came haftily to
me, and told me in my ear, that I had
obligations I little thought of to *Madamoifelle* XIII. that fhe had faid enough
to him to make him know fhe intended him for her confident, and added,
that fhe deferved I fhould make fome
return to her advances; and tho' he did
not enquire what had occafioned my
late melancholy, yet I could never meet
a better opportunity of diffipating it,
whence foever it proceeded. As I faid
                                    nothing

nothing to all this, he rejoined, that he would go that inftant to the *Chevalier*, and defire the ufe of his little pleafure-houfe, and offered to be at the whole expence of the fupper himfelf.

TAKING my filence for confent, he ran back to *Madamoifelle* XIII. and told her, that I joyfully accepted the plea-fure of fupping with her, then went a-bout the execution of all he had propofed. A moment's reflection on his behaviour, made me put this among the number of thofe things which might ferve to relieve my anxieties: as for the inclina-tion, he feemed to think *Madamoifelle* had for me, I looked upon it only as meer whim; but as I remembered her gaiety and good humour had very much plea-fed me, I was willing to try whether it would now have the fame effect. To-wards the end of the comedy, faw her lover with her in the balcony; the *Marquifs*, who having given his orders for the fupper, alfo returned at the fame time, and would needs have the ho-nour of inviting him himfelf: I joined

them

them immediately after, and we all went together in my coach.

Monsieur XXX. was master of the rolls, and his manner and behaviour pleased me extremely, nor did I find his wit less agreeable. At our arrival we perceived the *Chevalier* would not suffer the entertainment should be at our charge, and being come there with some of his friends, had made all necessary preparations.——Full of disquiet as my thoughts were, I made use of all my forces not to appear ridiculous by my gravity, among a company who were come entirely to devote themselves to mirth. The looks and complaisances of *Madamoiselle* XIII. persuaded me much more than the *Marquesses* words, that she had really some inclination for me ; and this obliging friend took care as we walked in the garden, frequently to draw her lover at some distance, and leave me near her. She made more advantage of these opportunities than I ; the little coquet omitted nothing that might assure me my addresses would not be unwelcome ; but I received all these

overtures

overtures with lefs of tendernefs, than politenefs.

When we fat down to table, the *Marquifs* placed me as favourably as he could; I was feated on her right hand, and her lover on her left, and the whole time of fupper fhe laid her foot on mine, and preffed it inceffantly with fo much vehemence, that I was very much perplexed in what manner to receive a declaration of this nature.— I was indeed, unwilling to return fuch preffures, for fear of engaging too far in the fport. I could not, however, avoid giving fometimes a fmile, and that was even too much, fince not taken in the fenfe I meant it. Great part of the night paft over, with a vaft gaiety in all the company except myfelf, who was under a violent conftraint, not to let any thing of my real trouble appear in my words or actions.

Before we parted, *Madamoifelle* XIII. found an opportunity to tell me, that having learned my lodgings from the old *Marquifs*, I might expect to hear from her next day. This promife

touched

touched me so little, that falling presently on the perpetual subject of my complaints, I past the remainder of the night in my ordinary imaginations. I was but just out of bed, when I received a visit from the *Marquiss*, and the first compliment he made me was, to congratulate himself on the good office he was come to do me. I should envy you, *continued he*, if I were of another age.---*Madamoiselle* XIII. is a charming creature.---And will be yours I see. I had till then looked on all this adventure as raillery, and I still talked of it as such to the *Marquiss*, from whom I took care always to conceal my unhappy secret; but he put into my hands the same instant a letter, saying it came from her: read it then your self, *said I*, that you may see I would hide nothing from you. He did as I desired, and the contents of this epistle were, that if I had the same sentiments for her with which she had flatter'd herself, I should find that the inclination she had to oblige me, had procured the means of our meeting that same night.---That I had nothing to do

but

but to come to her door a quarter of an hour past twelve, where her maid would be ready to receive, and conduct me to her.----Did I not say so, *cried the old Marquiss, embracing me with transport,* ----she is your own, and you are sure of the most beautiful girl in all *Paris.*

I now began to regard this affair with another eye.----In the firm resolution I had to forget madame *de B****, I could not procure a more agreeable diversion: besides I might hope at least, to deceive my senses and imagination; and I know not how far this hope might have carried me, if I had not reflected at the same time that *Madamoiselle* XIII. was the mistress of another, and that her lover was a very worthy man. I had no occasion to think twice on what I ought to do in this matter: it is very unhappy, *said I,* that I have not a little less abhorrence for injustice; for I can never consent to be guilty of usurping the right of another. He laughed heartily at my scruple. What a fancy is this! *cried he,* you scarce know her lover, yet think your self obliged to sacrifice

to him the sweetest pleasures of life. If
I had more intimacy with him, *replied
I, coldly*, I should hesitate yet less than
I do; because I look upon the seducing
the mistress of a friend, as the most base
of crimes: but it is sufficient for me to
know, that he has a right to expect fidelity from her, as he keeps and main-
tains her in so handsome a manner.---
A woman is certainly ungrateful and
treacherous, who wrongs the man from
whom she receives her bread; but a
man is yet more vile and contemptible,
who seeks pleasures of this nature at a-
nother persons expence.

The *Murquiss* was quite surprized to
hear me speak in this manner, and impatient to convince me I had a wrong no-
tion of such intrigues: as for right, *said he*,
it is my opinion that a woman who has
once forfeited her virtue, may be the
property of all mankind.---It is in this
as in religion, if you go out of the pale
of the church, it imports not which
way you take: you may be a *Calvinist*,
or a *Lutheran*, or any other sect, or
all of them, if you cease to be a *Ca-
tholic*.

tholic. Besides continued he, the custom of the world has long since ex-
ploded all these delicacies: those mistresses which seem the most regular,
have their favourites whom they see in
the absence of him that keeps them,
women of that sort are allowed two
lovers; one for interest, and the other
for inclination; and I dont see how it
can be a crime to indulge two passions,
so natural as tenderness, and the desire
of living at ease. She that has no o-
ther dowry than her charms, sells them
for her support: she makes some rich
man happy for his money, and would it
not be cruel to refuse her the priviledge
of making herself happy, also with the
man she likes. In fine, this point is so
clear, and so generally allowed, that no
man of sense who purchases the favours
he receives, expects to keep his mistress to himself.

I shall give no serious answer, *said*
I, to this long apology for injustice;
but with all imaginable gratitude for
the offers of *Madamoiselle* XIII. you
shall see what I write to her. I then
took

took a pen and ink, and wrote this short
anſwer.

" I acknowledge your merit, and
" am ſenſible of the value of the fa-
" vour you are pleaſed to offer ; but as
" I know that if I were under engage-
" ments with you, nothing would be
" more afflicting to me than to find you
" unfaithful. I cannot therefore think of
" expoſing that worthy man who loves
" you to a misfortune, which would
" make me die with grief, if I were in
" his place."

I ſent this letter immediately, in ſpite
of all the *Marquiſs* could urge againſt
it, who trembled he ſaid for the redi-
cule I ſhould incur from all who might
hear of my behaviour.   O ! my dear
Marquiſs, replied I, I have no fears of
that nature.---I acknowledge no judge
but that within my breaſt, which would
never pardon me the breach of honeſty,
even in the pleaſures of love.

THIS act of virtue coſt me little to
perform, for if I had accepted the pro-
poſal

posal of *Madamoiselle* XIII. the compliance had proceeded more from my
passion for another, than inclination for
herself; and when I considered more
upon it, it seemed a kind of prophanation of the purity of my desires. My
trouble however, stood in need of some
consolation, which I sought for in af-
semblies; in feasts; in hunting; in fine,
in every pleasure, and in every exercise;
but all without success; I only encreased the evil, by joining the fatigue
of the body, to that of the mind.

ONE night when I was going home
with my accustomed meditations, chance
brought me into the street, and before
the house of madame *de B* * * *. A
thousand times I had been tempted to
approach this temple which contained
the treasure of my soul, yet always had
courage to resist the impulse, which I
regarded as a traytor to my peace, and
an infringement on the bounds I had prescribed myself; but now the opportunity seemed to allow I should treat it
with somewhat more indulgence. The
night being dark, and few or no persons

fons paffing, I ordered my coach and
fervants to wait for me at the end of the
ftreet, and then returned alone to that
fatal houfe, which I confidered as the caufe
of all my torments.---As I drew near,
the air methought was enchanted, and
I breathed the moft ravifhing fweetnefs.---The illufions of an unhappy love
are not always black and heavy ; in the
midft of that trembling and confufion,
from which I could not defend myfelf,
I felt my blood circulate with more vigour, and my heart fluttered with lefs
grief than joy. I ftayed near an hour
attached by the fweet emotion, and lull-
ed into a forgetfulnefs of my pains, while
a thoufand flattering images of paft de-
lights prefented themfelves to my memory.----Heaven knows how long I
fhould continued thus, perhaps, till the
fun had rofe upon my folly, had not the
impatience of my people brought them
in fearch of me, in fpite of the commands I had given.

THIS hour of pleafure enjoyed with
the moft perfect innocence, feemed to
me fo precious, that I thought I might
often

often seek such consolations, since neither my own reason, nor the virtue of
madame *de B**** could suffer by it. As
I had seen that admirable woman at
church, why might I not see her there
again, to feast my eyes upon her charms,
and to recommend her to heaven as its
most perfect work, without being perceived by her: I thought I ought not to
deny myself a satisfaction, which could
offend no body, and which even she
herself would be ignorant of. I went to
sleep with these ideas, and waking with
the same, went to that church where I
before had seen her. Early as I was, I
had not been there three minutes when
she came, habited in a plain and negli-
gent manner, but adorned with all that
modesty, majesty, and sweetness, which I
had always seen in her, and which indeed
were inseparable from her. Had any one
observed my countenance, the situation
of my heart had doubtless been discovered; but I took care not to stir from
the corner where I had placed myself,
and which gave me a full and distinct view
of all her motions. I was not, however,
so lost in admiration, as not to be able

to

to turn from her towards the altar, and
offer up my prayers and vows in her behalf.   As she went out, my eyes pursued her till the crowd interrupted the
dear prospect; and when I saw her no
longer, could not resist going to sit down
in the chair she had placed herself in: I
stayed there a quarter of an hour, more
happy and more proud, than in the possession of the first throne in the universe.
These pleasing *matins*, made me impatient for the *vespers*, at which time I returned to the same place, enjoyed the
same blessings, and came home with the
same consolation.

While I was thus endeavouring by
various ways to mitigate the troubles of
my mind, Monsieur *de B****, sent almost every day to enquire after my health,
to which obliging messages, I always returned an answer, that I found no alteration. As I ordered my people to say I
was in bed, he was sometime before he
was undeceived : but some accident at
last discovered to him, that I went out
every day, and that no other mark of infirmity than a profound melancholy was
                              observed

observed in me. I frequently fent my *valet de chamber* with my compliments to him and his lady; but though I had dictated to him what replies he fhould make to any queftions might be afked him, yet I am not fure he might not at fometimes be too little prepared, with the evafions neceffary to preferve my fecret; but I know that whenever he came back, I did not fail of interrogating him on every particular relating to madame *de B****, I would make him tell me if fhe was at home.---What fhe was doing.---What fhe faid.---How fhe looked.------ How fhe was dreft, and if fhe feemed gay, or penfive.---The leaft circumftances were highly material to me. He told me that he always found her in her hufband's chamber, that when he went to the bedfide, fhe drew near to hear the compliments he brought, but left to Monfieur *de B**** the care of anfwering them without fpeaking one fingle word herfelf.

AFTER having proved by a multitude of effays, that tumultuous affemblies, nor the noife and pomp of public fhews shews, made no change in the situation of my mind. I returned to those societies with which the *President* had brought me acquainted. The company of persons whose wit was under the direction of their judgment, and whose judgment was always accompanied with benevolence and good manners, flattered my taste for all that was virtuous and amiable. As I was continually introduced to new acquaintance of this sort, I now began to regard *Paris* as the most elegant city in the world, and condemned myself for having entertained an opinion of the whole, on the model I had seen on my first arrival at the house of madame the *Intendant*'s lady, and others of her companions. It is true, the number of the wise and good, are few in comparison, with those of a contrary manner of thinking and behaviour; but then those few excell so much, all that I have found in any other place, as to acquire this city the reputation it so justly deserves, not only all over *Europe*, but the world.

THAT air of melancholy which I could not throw off, affected those worthy

thy companies to which I now reforted: I received every moment fome proofs of this tender compaffion; but far from thinking to eafe my forrows by giving vent to them, I evaded all queftions put to me for that end. The fame reafon which had made me quit monfieur and madame *de B * * **, made me careful my fecret fhould not even be gueffed at. I thought it fhameful to confefs a paffion which I very well knew my duty obliged me to combat with all my might; and befides, as none but myfelf could be a proper judge of the nature of my fentiments, and the purity of my flame, I feared the leaft explication would be an injuftice to my character, and alfo to the honour of the woman I adored. And this it was which hindered me from opening my mind, even to my beft friend monfieur *de la * * **, from whom I kept nothing elfe concealed. The intereft he took in my affairs, made him often prefs me with the moft tender concern to place that confidence in him, which he faid his zeal to ferve me demanded: the *Marchionefs* alfo his

E   kinfwo-

kinfwoman, who had no lefs friendfhip for me, made me the fame in-
ftances; but I defended myfelf againft
all their folicitations, and anfwered only by my fighs, which augmented their
difquiet and furprife.

For three weeks my chief confola-
tion was the feeing madame *de B* * * *
at church, and in paffing good part of
the night before her door. Her hufband was now convinced that it was
not bad health kept me from his houfe,
fince I could go every day to others,
and having ftudied my temper and principles enough to confide in the friendfhip I had for him, took a refolution
to force me out of that forgetfulnefs I
feemed to have of the fentiments he
had a thoufand times teftified in my favour. He wrote a letter to me, full
of invitations, and the moft tender reproaches for my long abfence; but
what caufed in me the greateft aftonifhment, was to find at the bottom
of the letter, two or three lines of madame *de B* * *'s hand-writing, her hufband having told me above, that to
give

give greater weight to his entreaties, he had defired his wife to add fomething of her own.

NOTHING could be more fimple than this invitation of madame *de B* * * *. She told me that if I were capable of any gratitude for my friends, I would not fuffer her hufband to languifh any longer in the impatience of feeing me, and that fhe willingly gave me this advice for his fatisfaction. Capable of gratitude, *cried I!* ah how little do you know my heart! then, after reading it again, for his fatisfaction. Alas! *rejoined I,* it is only in his fatisfaction you intereft yourfelf: all befides is indifferent to you. Refpect, adoration, you think nothing of in any other, you perceive nothing!——You fpeak of gratitude, yet are yourfelf capable of feeling none for him who dies for you. The violence of my paffion was fuch, as forced even the tears from my eyes. I had not power to refift the command fhe gave me, however, and as I went, recollected one word which foothed the difquiets which the others had oc-

cafioned. I give you this advice willingly. She will not then, *faid I*, be
offended that I execute it. She will
fee me without pain. She will fuffer
me without regret. In this mad fa-
fhion did my paffion argue, yet I fo-
lemnly profefs my fentiments were not
in the leaft changed, nor my wifhes
more guilty than before. But I found
afterwards, that this vifit very much
encreafed my malady, and rendered my
fituation lefs fupportable.

THE lively fatisfaction that monfieur
de B * * * teftified at feeing me enter,
proved more than ever the affection he
had for me. His wife was retired, it
feems, he had defired fhe would not
be prefent when I came, that he might
have more liberty to exprefs his joy. I
was not forry to find her abfent in the
firft moment, becaufe I was apprehen-
five the diforder of my heart might have
been difcoverable, either in my looks
or fpeech. After fome difcourfe, full
of tendernefs, monfieur *de B* * * * preffed me in the moft ferious terms to explain the motive of my long abfence.
                                You

You have a regard for me, I am certain, *said he*, and are sensible of the friendship I have for you. Nor do I think you hate my wife, *continued he, fixing his eyes intently on my face*, to what then am I to impute these three weeks absence and forgetfulness of us? As I begun to lay the excuse on ill health, and a hurry of business, you do not deal sincerely with me, *interrupted he*, and I see the perplexity my curiosity has involved you in; but will you pardon me if I take the liberty of guessing at some part of your sentiments? I could not reply to this question, I promised, however, to grant what he desired. You are in love, *said he*, I have discovered it a long time ago. My confusion redoubling at these words, *he added without giving me time to recover myself*, you are in love with my wife.

THOUGH the tone in which he spoke had nothing in it resentful, the uncertainty I was in of his intention, kept me from making him any direct reply. How, monsieur! *cried I*, if I had ever failed in that respect, due to ma-

E 3   dame

dame *de B * * *,* I fhould never forgive myfelf. Be under no difcompo-
fure my dear *Count, faid he, with a
fmile.* But I know your delicacy, and
that I have touched you in the tender-
eft part. Then continued to affure me
with the fame freedom, that we were
not three days acquainted, before he
had difcovered the fecret of my heart,
that far from being alarmed at it, he
had taken pleafure to obferve the pro-
grefs of my paffion, that he had pitied
the conftraint I had put upon myfelf;
that my pretended indifpofition had not
deceived him one moment;---and that
having judged by my melancholy, the
terrible conflict I endured between my
honour and the impulfe of my inclination, he had admired the ftrength of
my virtue and my refolution ;---that the
day I took leave of him, he was feve-
ràl times about to tell me, that love
and jealoufy were not the paffions of a
dying man ;---that fully convinced, as
he was of the purity and integrity of
madame *de B * * *,* he found nothing
to condemn in the admiration I had of
her ; that the character I had in the
world,

world, and the good opinion he had
of my principles, had also assured him,
he had nothing to apprehend ;---that he
did not wonder more how I could force
myself to endure so long an absence
from her, than that he had been able
to support mine ; that in this situation,
a friend like myself, was no less dear
to him than his wife, and that his
heart put no difference between us. In
fine, giving me his hand with the utmost tenderness, my dear *Count, said
he,* I call heaven to witness of the confidence I have in your honour, and the
virtue of my wife. I do not blame
your passion : she is worthy of all the
attachment you have for her : love her
then, you have her husband's permission ; but let me come in for a part of
this happiness, and inflict neither on
yourself or me, the pains of any more
such absences for the future.

I imagine, *added he,* that she cannot
be ignorant of your passion, because
your eyes so visibly betray it ; but I
have discovered nothing in either of
you, that should make me think she

knows

knows it by any other way. Am
I miftaken or not? *rejoined be a
little more gay than before*, tell me without referve. I had liftened to him till
then, with an aftonifhment which had
rendered me incapable of interrupting
him, but rouzed by this queftion, I
took his hand, and prefling it between
mine, ah! *faid I with a figh*, that I
love madame *de B* * * *, is but too fad
a truth, and that I refpect her as heaven itfelf, is no lefs true---do juftice
to the fentiments I have for her, fince
you have penetrated into them---be affured alfo, that I have fuffered the torments of abfence no lefs through the
fears of offending you than her---that I
have not a friend in the world for whom
I have a more fincere or tender regard
than for yourfelf---that my cruel paffion never infpired me with one fingle
wifh, which if known, you could con-
demn---that it has in it more of an
ætherial, than a grofs earthly nature,
that I love madame *de B* * * *, no lefs
for that confummate virtue I firmly believe her miftrefs of, than for thofe inimitable perfections which fhine about
                                    her

her person---that I love her also as she
is yours, a part of yourself---doubt not
then of the inviolable affection I have
for you, or that my soul does not
avow to be the best, the most generous
of mankind, the most worthy of madame *de B****. Yes, *added I*, you
may safely depend on my honour, and
the sanctity of my principles, nor less
on her virtue, in trials to which one
cannot imagine it should ever be exposed, on my account, at least, who am
far from flattering myself with the most
distant thought of ever making any impression on her heart. I don't know
that, *replied he laughing*, the women
have the art to conceal such things, as
they are sensible we cannot find out,
without their own confession ; and I
dare say, you will not expect I should
endeavour to wrest such a secret from
her breast, to tell it again to you.

WHILE he was thus turning the adventure into merriment, I was taken
up with a reflection, which in the
abundance of my heart, I communi-
cated to him. Alas! *cried I*, you make

E 5   me

me the happieſt of mankind, with leſs
riſque to yourſelf, than my own innocence. But tell me what countenance
I ſhall be able to wear before you,
when being ſo often here as I propoſe,
and you have the goodneſs to deſire, I
muſt ſupport the looks of madame *de
B* * * *, and of yours at the ſame time.
It is myſelf, *replied he*, that would have
the moſt difficult part to act in this affair, if I had leſs confidence in my wife
or in you, this thought had cauſed
me ſome pain, and in the joy I found
in being relieved from it by his anſwer,
I kiſſed his hand with little leſs tenderneſs than I ſhould have done that of his
wife. Ah! *ſaid I, in the ſame tranſport*, why then is the happineſs you
grant me delayed?---why is ſhe not
here?--- ſhe, who is accuſtomed to be
always near you? He rung his bell at
theſe words, and madame *de B* * * *,
who was reading in the next room, ran
haſtily in, imagining he wanted ſomething.

AT her approach, all heaven methought ſeemed opened to me, after
having

having eagerly gazed on her, as if my eyes had apprehended some change in her. I found voice to addreſs her with a timid compliment: ſhe anſwered with more freedom, yet had a reſerve in her air, which ſeemed alſo to denote ſhe was not wholly free from perplexity. Her husband to whom I turned my head in order to conſult his countenance, I could perceive obſerved us with much attention. He was the firſt, however, that broke the ſilence we were falling into, by telling his wife, that I had pro-miſed to be more aſſiduous in my viſits: the converſation between us began by degrees to be entirely eaſy till dinner time, for it was before noon I went there. I ſeated myſelf at the table without ſtay-ing for being aſked : it is true, that two plates were laid, and Monſieur *de B**** had ſeemed to deſire my company by his eyes. I could not forbear being ſur-prized however at my own familiarity ; I now alſo eat with an appetite, and Madame *de B****, who had never ſeen me do ſo before, congratulated me on the perfect recovery of my health. I did not attempt to penetrate into the mean-

ing

ing of her words, which might be underſtood two ways: but I was enchanted to ſee and hear her.---I frequently
caſt my eyes on her huſband, to teſtifie
the tranſport I was in, and ſometimes
alſo with apprehenſions, that the ſight of
it ſhould make him repent his promiſes.

BUT on the contrary perceiving he en-
couraging me by all the ſigns of good humour and approbation, my heart exalted,
and my gaiety encreaſed. I had remarked
that at ſitting down at table, Madame
de B***, had alſo ſeemed rather more
full of vivacity, than ever I had ſeen in
her; theſe appearances perſuading me at
leaſt that ſhe ſaw me without diſguſt,
contributed to ſupport that air of joy,
which rendered me another man than I
was at the laſt viſit I had made there.
But I ſoon perceived that her ſprightli-
neſs diminiſhed by degrees: in vain I
endeavoured to ſee into the motive of
this change: ſhe carefully avoided even
looking towards me, and became ſo
mute, and in a manner ſullen, that it
was with difficulty I obtained the leaſt
word in anſwer to any thing I ſaid, and
what

what she spoke was so reserved and cold,
as shewed me that what little she contributed to the conversation, was only
extorted from her by her good manners.
I examined seriously what I had done to
deserve her hate, or her contempt, and
could accuse myself with nothing; at
last I imagined she had over-heard the
discourse had past between me and her
husband, and that her virtue was alarmed at it. This reflection, and the fear of
having displeased her, threw me in my
turn into the most profound meditation;
all my gaiety abandoned me, and I became sad and speechless, even to draw
upon me many reproaches from Monsieur *de B****; when all on a sudden
by a strange revolution, the eyes of his
wife began to sparkle, as mine grew
dull, and her good humour returned in
proportion with my heaviness. This second alteration gave me a fresh subject
of agitation; I knew not how to judge
of those strange vicissitudes.---Can this
woman, *said I to myself*, whom I
thought so superior to all the weakness
of her sex, be capable of caprice?---Can
all those adorable perfections be sullied
with

with any of the little arts of coquetry.—
Thus did I for a moment injure the
brighteſt mind that ever was lodged in
humane clay; but what elſe could I
think. I durſt not flatter myſelf that it
was any tender emotions on my account
which had engroſt her thoughts.—It was
not in the nature of my principles, nor
the awful reſpect I paid her to be ſo vain.
Happy was it for me, that I was not,
if any thing in ſo perplexing a circumſtance as mine can be called ſo.—I am
obliged to acknowledge my want of penetration at that time, as the goodneſs
of heaven to me; ſince not only my innocence, my repoſe, but even my life
demanded I ſhould yet longer continue
in ignorance, of what paſſed in the heart
of that excellent woman: the misfortunes which fell on me the following
night, had too much triumphed over
my conſtancy, if I had known all the
good they had deprived me of.

T H E remainder of the day, and all
the evening, was paſt in a mixture of
play and converſation. Monſieur *de*
B * * *, loved *Piquet*, we made a party,

ty, and feated our felves as commodi-
oufly as we could for his fituation. The
opportunity which looking over her
cards, or fhewing her mine, gave of
contemplating her charms more nearly,
afforded me a profufion of delight; but
I was furprized that after leaving play,
Monfieur *de B * * **, defired me to relate to him the particulars of an inci-
dent, which I thought had been unknown to all the world. The intereft I
took in your health, *faid he*, making
me inquifitive in what manner you paft
your time: I heard you was feen at a
fale of goods, belonging to *M. Y. D. Y.*
that you bought nothing, yet feemed
very much concerned in the difpofal of
them, and I was told alfo, *continued he*,
that this honeft *Advocate* was immediately after reftored to all his misfortunes had compelled him to part with.
I found by this difcourfe, that he was
very well acquainted with the whole affair, and replied that I was forry the
gratitude of *M. Y. D. Y.* had made
him betray my fecret; that I would have
taken more care to conceal it from him,
if I apprehended a difcovery; but fince
the

the thing was done, it would be now in vain to deny it.

I t was meer chance, *said I,* that informed me *M. Y. D. Y.* had been ruined by various misfortunes; that his creditors had drove him to the extremity of felling all that former ill accidents had left him. Every one fpoke of him as a perfect honeft man, and pittied the fad ftate of his affairs; having a family of children all unprovided for, and without means of receiving any education, that could enable them to fupport themfelves; fo that if during his life, they might receive a wretched fuftenance by his bufinefs, after his death they could be no better than beggars. The ftory moved me very much, I mentioned it to feveral perfons of my acquaintance, and who alfo knew him, but found all I faid excited no more than a barren compaffion: not one among them all feemed willing to contribute any thing to the relief of a diftrefs they could but lament. I made fome reflections on the hardnefs of hearts, and without communicating my intentions to any one, I went directly

rectly to enquire farther into the character of *M. Y. D. Y.* and having found it irreproachable, set me down to consider what I could do for him. Besides the estate left me by my uncle, I found a considerable sum of ready money in his coffers : fourscore thousand *livres*, of which were yet remaining in the hands of a *Notary Public*, with whom I had lodged them. I thought I could not dispose of this money better, than in the relief of merit in distress, and was about to send it immediately to him ; but being informed that his effects were already seized, and the sale appointed on the next day : I formed another plan, which I thought would be less liable to discovery, for I always thought that actions of this nature, lose all their merit if divulged. I found his estate consisted of a piece of land of fifteen hundred livres yearly rent ; two houses at *Paris*, with some plate and furniture, and I employed three persons to be the purchasers, but separately, and under feigned names ; I was present at the sale, but it was only to prevent being imposed upon,

upon, either by the creditors, or my own people.

My agents bought the land and houfes, for fixty thoufand livres, and the furniture for five thoufand. The fums were paid before night, and the impatience I had to relieve *M. Y. D. Y.* out of that defpair, in which he muft neceffarily be plunged, made me fend him that fame evening the contracts of fale, with the acquittances of all his creditors, accompanied with a little billet, in which I told him, that I found an infinite pleafure in having the means of obliging him, and conjured him not to interrupt it by making any enquiries who I was. At the return of my *Notary*, who I had charged with this commiffion, I was aftonifhed to fee him bring back the contracts and acquittances; he told me alfo the anfwer of the *Advocate*, who had been very importunate with him to know my name. It feems the tranfports of his furprize and gratitude, had rendered him incapable of retaining any moderation. Take my eftate, *faid he*, take my life, and that of all my children;

dren; but deny me not the knowledge of so god-like a man. The *Notary* persisting in obeying the injunction I had laid upon him; the other in conducting him to the door, forced him to take back the papers, and as he turned away, said, I never will accept such cruel benefits, as refuse me the power of loving the saviour of my life.

I thought myself too much recompenced, in having excited such tender emotions. Return, *said I to the Notary*, and without the least explication, leave the papers upon the table. But this way succeeded no better than the other: the *Notary* came back without having the precaution to observe if he was followed; while he was given me an account of what he had done, I saw a man of a very venerable aspect, aged about sixty, and habited as an *Advocate*, come into my chamber. Here he is himself, *cried the Notary*, but I had no need of being told who he was. This honest man would have thrown himself at my feet, if my superior agility had not prevented him. Ah! *said he with tears in his*
eyes,

eyes, conceal no longer from me my ſaviour and redeemer from all worldly miſeries; if you refuſe my adorations, permit me at leaſt to lock you in my arms. I cannot expreſs what my heart felt in that moment.---A ſatisfaction almoſt too great to bear over-flowed it.-- He held me a long time, embraced and preſſed me with all his force. I heard and felt his ſighs, and the tenderneſs with which I was myſelf diſſolved at the motions I obſerved in him, deprived me alſo of the power of ſpeech.

I am not yet at the end of this ſcene: he had brought his three children, haveing prevailed on my ſervants to let them ſtay in the anti-chamber: a girl about ſixteen or ſeventeen; a boy of fifteen, and another of ten or twelve years old. He quitted my arms without ſaying one word, and running to the door made a ſign to them to advance. Kneel, *ſaid be to them*, kneel all of you my children, and behold the man whom next to god, you are to love and honour your whole lives.--- It is he who gives you the means of living, and is more than father to you.

you. They were so ready to obey him, that I was not able to prevent them, and besides the spectacle was too moving for a heart like mine. I was quite overcome, in so much as I was obliged to throw myself into an easy chair, and having made a sign to the *Notary* to raise the children : cease, cease, *said I to the father*, to cause in me such agitations, as surpass all my forces to sustain.----A gratitude like this is infinitely beyond the benefit.----You even take from me all the merit of my bounty, by proving that what I have done for such a person as yourself, was no more than bare duty.

By degrees, however, the violence of the first transports abated, and we entered into discourses more coherent; I acquainted *M. Y. D. Y.* with the way by which I was made acquainted with his misfortunes, after which, perceiving his daughter was very amiable, I asked him if he had yet thought of disposing her in marriage ? to which he answered, that in the state of her fortune, of which I had saved the remains, they must

muſt wait for more happy circumſtances.
As I had ſtill fifteen thouſand livres of
the fourſcore, I had deſigned to his ſervice, I prevailed on him, after a long
reſiſtance, to permit me to beſtow it on
her for a dowry. I alſo queſtioned him
concerning his eldeſt ſon, and found,
that the diſorder of his affairs had o-
bliged him to take him from the college. I then offered to take him into
my company, and join ſomething to
the king's pay, for his ſubſiſtence. If
he anſwers the good opinion I have of
him, *ſaid I,* and proves himſelf worthy
of his father, I will engage to make
him my cornet, in order to bring him
by degrees into other commiſſions.

THUS I had the pleaſure of making
a worthy family perfectly at eaſe ; without thinking I merited any extraordinary praiſe, ſince I had only ſacrificed a
ſuperfluity, a ſum which I could very
well ſpare, but fortune apart ; I believe
if one could compare ſentiment with ſentiment, I verily believe, that *M. Y. D.
Y.* felt not more ſatisfaction at ſeeing
himſelf and credit re-eſtabliſhed, than

I

I did in having been the inftrument of his being fo.

MONSIEUR and Madame *de B* * * *, loaded me encomiums, fuch as I could not think I deferved for following only the motives of my own inclinations ; but I was not difpleafed that this affair had confirmed the high idea the hufband had of my principles, and could not help feeling an extreme fatisfaction in the teftimonies I received of the wifes efteem. Love has this effect on generous fouls, it makes them endeavour to pleafe by the exercife of all the virtues in their power. I could not have been capable of informing Madame *de B****, of any thing which might have ingratiated myfelf with her ; but muft acknowledge I was fenfible of the moft lively joy that the teftimonies of others, and a confeffion wrefted as it were from myfelf, had made fo great an impreffion on her.

THIS was a day of blifs, but in the conclufion of it, fortune began to declare openly her malice to me, and let
fly

fly all thofe fhafts fhe had for fometime
been preparing againft me. I left the
houfe of Monfieur *de B****, a little
before midnight, I was in my chair and
had only one footman with me: All
was quiet in the ftreets when I heard
the voice of a man biding my chairmen
ftop: on which I afked what he would
have with me; and he civilly defiring
to fpeak a word or two with me in private. I went out in order to know his
bufinefs.

THE darknefs of the night, *faid he*,
hinders you from knowing me, I am
St. *V****. I then remembered his voice,
he was brother of that young lady my
father had intended for his wife, and
whofe pretended claim on me had
given me fo much vexation. Ha! *cried
I*, you are welcome to *Paris*; I am extremely glad to fee you here. It depends on you, *replied he coldly*, to make
me find the fame fatisfaction in feeing
you.---You may eafily comprehend, *continued he*, the reafons which have brought
me here. He then told me, that having
been in garrifon at *Strasburgh*, he had
been

been ignorant of the proceedings between me and his sister : that some unseasonable fears had prevented his family from acquainting him, but that one of his friends having been more communicative, he was astonished to find what had passed in his absence ; in a word, there was no occasion for him to make a detail of my actions, but came to demand a more perfect account of them from myself.

I shall refuse you nothing on this point, answered I, and your perplexity will be soon over, if you are disposed to believe me. I then recited to him the whole adventure, omitting nothing relating to my father, his sister, or myself, even to my very thoughts on the strange pretensions she had made, and concluded with all the asseverations of a man of honour, that I had not swerved in the least article from truth. I do not suspect you of any imposition, *returned he*, and hope you will do me the same justice : but my honour suffers in that of my sister ; the public censure is a tyrant,

F and

and you know to what meafures your refufal obliges me, in fpite of myfelf.

BESIDES the averfion I had for duels, I knew *St. V**** to be a good natured fenfible man, and had always very much efteemed him.   I therefore made ufe of many arguments, in which heaven knows, I had reafon and juftice on my fide, to perfuade him that he had not the leaft caufe of complaint againft me.----I repeated to him even the fcruples I had within myfelf, and that I had fubmitted the cafe to judges whofe opinion was incapable of being byaffed. He made but one reply to all I faid, but it was fuch as fhewed me he had taken his refolution. Independant of his own ideas of the matter, *he faid*, he found himfelf compelled by a fevere neceffity, either to kill his friend, or be killed by him. That the officers of his corps were informed of our difference, that it was become the public difcourfe; and that he came to *Paris* in fearch of me. His fifters reputation, and the honour of his family muft be retrieved, and he had only to hear from my mouth, *yes*, or *no*. You have
al-

already heard, *replied I*, that I am not
at liberty, having sworn to abide by the
decision I have mentioned. But *added*
I, will not the explanation I have given
you satisfy your corps? No, *cried he*,
and drawing his sword, bid me defend
myself. I told him I took mine with
regret, and on this we began a combat,
which was the more dangerous, as we
engaged in it without passion, and without hate.--St. *V* * * * aimed at my life,
I was no less resolute to defend it, but at
the same time, careful to avoid giving
him any mortal wound : I directed my
thrusts chiefly at his sword arm, which
gave him great advantage over me, especially, as the half extinguished light
of a distant lanthorn happened to be
full on me, while he remained in a kind
of shade. He gave me a wound in the
side, I returned it with one in the arm,
but did not perceive it had abated his
strength, and in the mean time received
a very deep wound myself, in the lower
belly, on which fearing the loss of blood
would render me unable to maintain the
combat, I exerted my whole strength
and skill, and pierced him so unluckily

in

in the arm, juſt above the bend, that my ſword entered one ſide of his breaſt. His ſword fell that inſtant out of his hand; and I ſet my foot upon it, in order to hear what he would ſay, but ſaw him fall immediately after.

I now called my people, who were about ſome thirty paces diſtant; I have need of aſſiſtance *ſaid I*, but will not receive it till after you have carried my enemy to the firſt ſurgeon, by good fortune they found one in the ſame ſtreet, to whom they conveyed him. St. *V** was not dead, as I took care to aſſure myſelf by the beating of his pulſe, but was deprived of all ſenſe and motion, and in that condition left to the help of art. As for myſelf, I reſolved to depend on my *valet de chambre*, whoſe ſkill in ſurgery my father had often warranted, after having had him twenty years in his ſervice; ſo went into my chair, and did not faint, nor loſe any part of my preſence of mind, either then, or in the dreſſing of my wounds.

I

I had not fpoke one word, after having ordered the chairmen to carry me
home, and was fallen on the end of fo
bloody a combat, into the fame coldnefs with which I had drawn my fword;
but why do I fay coldnefs, it was rather a ftupidity, which the force of my
reflections foon drew me out of, and
threw me into the moft black and horrid melancholy. What a crowd of dif-
mal ideas then all at once took poffeffion of my brain! innocent, or guilty,
faid I to myfelf, to what a wretched
cataftrophe am I brought, without having the leaft fore-warning of it! my
fate is come all at once upon me! indeed, *continued I with fighs that almoft
cleft my heart*, I have many times feared I was born to be unhappy; my
paffion for madame *de B* * * has already inflicted mortal torments on me,
and even in the change which has happened this day in my favour, I fee my
pains will yet be much greater than my
pleafures: the very nature of my attachment makes me tremble. She is
married! ah how unjuft, how pernici-

F 3   ous

ous to my honour and my principles, how detestable even to my own wishes is a flame which cannot be satisfied but by invading the rights of another! and trampling down all religious, and all moral ties! Then my humour which I every day find more and more different from the generality of mankind, has given me little felicity in most of the society I meet with. What advantages have I made of youth, of birth, of fortune? What real pleasures have I been capable of enjoying, all that are called so, either are too gross, or my taste is too refined? all the perspective behind me affords nothing to delight the mind. What then is that before me. Dreadful! amazing! I am forced in my defence to kill a gallant man, my friend, and to return home covered with my own blood. With what horrors am I not threatened! sure I am destined by heaven to fill the number of those who are celebrated for their misfortunes, and to astonish the whole world by my miseries or my crimes.

WHILE

WHILE a thousand black presages of those ills which since have fallen on me, ran in my distracted mind. My *valet de chambre*, in whom I had all the confidence his zeal and sincerity deserved, came to ask me if I was certain my adventure would not be known, and if it were not proper he should take some measures for my safety. This remonstrance, which was indeed very seasonable, made me consider, where it would be most proper to address for advice and assistance. The tender friendship in which I was united with Monsieur *de la* * * *, made me look upon him as the person who would be most ready to forgive being disturbed in the dead of night. I therefore sent my chairmen directly to him, with orders to bring him, if he were so good to permit them. My message was no sooner delivered to him, then he quited his bed, threw on his night-gown, and put on his slippers, and flew to me with all the impatience of the most ardent good will.

ASSOON

ASSOON as a faw him on my bed-side, you find me, *faid I,* in a very unhappy ftate, yet more fo by the agitations of my mind, than by the wounds I have received. The chairmen had told him, that it was returning from the houfe of monfieur *de* ***B, I had encountered my enemy, which, together with my words, made him imagine the accident had happened on the fcore of that lady. Ah! *cried he,* I now no longer wonder at the change of your behaviour. Madame *de B* * * * is capable of infpiring a very great paffion. I now not doubting but he had difcovered my fecret, forgot not only the fmart of my wounds, but alfo the occafion on which I had fent for him, and thought of nothing but vindicating the innocence of madame *de B* * * *, againft the falfe reports had been fpread of her, the purity of my own defires, and the miftery I had made of them to the beft of friends. Thefe three points engaged me in a long difcourfe, which even I know not when I fhould have broke off, if Monfieur *de la* ***, fur-

prized

prized at what he heard, had not interrupted me, by telling me, my fituation did not permit me to fpeak fo
much.

He could not, however, refrain afk-
ing me a queftion, which, to anfwer,
put my heart into the extremeft palpi-
tation. After having expreffed his aftonifhment at the excefs and delicacy of
my paffion, as alfo at the extraordinary
condefcenfion I had received from monfieur *de B* ***; and do you think, *faid
he*, that his wife has not the fame like-
ing for you, as you have teftified for
her? I muft confefs this demand rendered me unable to contain myfelf; like-
ing, *cried I*, ah give a better name to
a flame pure and diffinterefted as that
of the angelic beings. The admiration,
the tendernefs which is infpired by a
woman of merit, is an invincible af-
cendant, an empire, a defpotic power
over the foul, and all its faculties. I
may like a thoufand amiable women,
but madame *de B* * * *, alone, has
taught me what it is to love. If you
afk if fhe has a fort of liking for me, I

F 5 flatter

flatter myſelf ſhe has. Her goodneſs, perſuades me of it; but you are widely miſtaken, if you think ſhe feels the ſame for me, I do for her. No, that would be to confound a bare eſteem and good-will, with the moſt violent paſſion that ever was.

MONSIEUR de la ***, was a very worthy man, and wholly free from the corruption of the times; but ſome experiences he had met with in an unlucky engagement, had very much prejudiced him againſt the fair ſex, and that exceſs of tenderneſs I teſtified, ſeemed to him no better than a ridiculous blindneſs; however, he confeſſed, that what he called liking, might be in a greater or leſs degree, in proportion to the warmth of the conſtitution, or the merit of the object; but he could not depart from the opinion that Madame de B *** had an inclination for me: he was certain of it, he ſaid, even from the deſcription I had given of her conduct, and her behaviour to me; that ſhe waited only for the declaration of my ſentiments, to anſwer to them, with

with all the liberty her hufband feemed to authorize, and that fhe, doubtlefs, fuffered much by my too timid
delay. In fine, he fet no bounds to
his ideas, and reproached me for making no more advantage of the tendernefs of fo beautiful a woman, efpecially at a time when fhe was in a manner
loft to the world, by her conftant at-
tendance on a fick man. You are more
penetrating then I, *added he,* and are
better able to judge whether it is intereft
or affection, that has attached her fo
ftrongly to her hufband; but I will undertake to aver, that it depends wholly on yourfelf after your recovery, to
triumph over both the one and the
other.

I had liftened to this difcourfe with
a great deal of impatience, had it come
from one I lefs loved, perhaps, I fhould
have preferved more moderation; for
I know that the generality of mankind,
are to apt to judge of the whole, by
the example of fome few illuftrious
falfe ones, who are a difhonour to their
fex, but I was afflicted to find the dear-

eſt of my friends governed by a prepoſ-
ſeſſion I thought ſo unworthy of his
character. Be aſſured, *ſaid I*, that I
have of madame *de B****, the
opinion that I have declared to you,
and that it is no leſs to her virtue, than
her beauty, I have ſurrendered my heart,
were the firſt of theſe perfections to fail
in her, my paſſion for the other would
be ſoon extinguiſhed. I ſhall therefore
never ſollicit for an advantage, which
I ſhould be ſorry to procure, and perhaps refuſe if offered. For it is, and
ever ſhall be an eſtabliſhed maxim with
me, that whatever paſſion I am capable of for a woman, I ſhould never aſk
any thing that ſhould infringe the fidelity of her engagements, if ſhe loves
her huſband, or the unqueſtionable rights
of her huſband, if ſhe does not love
him.

THE low idea Monſieur *de la ****
had entertained of love, as it was ordinarily conducted, did not hinder him
from having the moſt exalted notions
of all the virtues. He could not refuſe
his approbation to my ſentiments, and
only

only dwelt on the difficulty of finding
such a woman as I had described madame *de B***,* though all, indeed,
said he, ought to be such, both for the
happiness of themselves and us; for
where is the man that would not adore,
when virtue and beauty were united?
but perceiving so long a conversation
had a little altered me, he prayed me
to tell him how my wounds and my
passion agreed. On which I reflected
that my zeal had carried me too far,
and wondered at myself, for having delayed giving him some account of my
tragical adventure. I had before acquainted him with the pretensions of
Madamoiselle *St. V.* ***, and I now no
sooner named her brother than he
comprehended the occasion of our quarrel; but having carefully related to him
all the circumstances of the duel, which
could be verified by three witnesses, he
agreed with me, that I had no need of
absenting myself, since what I had done
was so manifestly in my own defence.
I then pressed him to return, but he
absolutely refused to quit me till the
next morning, that he might judge of
the

the danger of my wounds, by feeing
the firft dreffing taken of. You fee,
faid I, fmiling, that a fincere affection
is capable of attaching a perfon in perfect health, to the bed of the fick.   Let
then your own example infpire you
with a little more indulgence for o-
thers.

HE paffed the remainder of the
night in an eafy chair, and about nine
o'clock in the morning a loud knocking
at the door obliged him to go and order there fhould be lefs noife.   I had
two anti-chambers, and he had paffed
the firft, when he faw an officer of
juftice with fome mufquetiers entering
the fecond: all my people, except the
porter who attended the gate, were
lain down to fleep, fo they found an
eafy admittance. The fight of Monfieur
de La * * * in a night cap and gown,
made them fuppofe it was myfelf.   I
have orders, *faid the officer*, to arreft,
and conduct you to *Fort L'Evecque*; I
hope you will not oblige us to have recourfe to force. Monfieur *de La* * * *,
eafily comprehended it was for me they
came,

came, and with as much presence of
mind as friendship, took the advantage
of their mistake to supply my place;
he awaked my *Valet de Chambre*, and
in two words made him see into his design; — then desiring leave to dress himself, he ordered my cloaths to be brought,
which was done, even to my very shoes,
and behaved himself so exactly like the
master of the apartment, that none had
the least suspicion of his being a stranger.
While he was putting on the things,
he said in a careless manner, that he
was surprized to find himself arrested
for an affair, in which he found nothing of
guilt; it will then be more easy for you
to justifie yourself, *said the officer*. My
servants being all up by this time, he affected to give orders to each; and asked
the officer if he might not be permitted to take one along with him, which
being granted, he found means to tell
my *valet de chambre* that he would not
have me lose a moment till I had put
myself in some place where I might be
concealed; and then discending surrounded by the guards, went into a
hackney coach which they had brought
for

for him to the door. The servant he took with him was a discreet sober man, and had served me a long time.

THE moment they were gone, my *valet de chambre* came in to wake me: my sleep had not been so sound, but that I thought I heard some sort of bustle in the *anti-chamber*: I presently asked for Monsieur *de La* * *, and was surprized at being told what had happened. Though I apprehended no danger for my friend in the service he had rendered me, I regretted he should suffer even a moment on my account.———Secure as I was in my own innocence, I thought it ungenerous to let him remain in prison, when the worst that could befall me, was only being confined there somewhat longer than he would be, without surrendering myself; and this fear would never have prevented me from going that moment to exchange place with him, if my *valet de chambre* had not represented to me, that my wounds required an other kind of regimen, than I could have in a prison. In taking off the dressing he found the hurt I had received

ceived in the lower belly, was more dangerous than he had apprehended, and stood in need of the greatest precautions. I consented to his prescriptions, but the troubles of my mind admitted no relief.

THE advice Monsieur *de La* **, had left for my concealing myself, seemed to imply that I must quit *Paris,* for where could I have been screened in that city? and to go from it, was to abandon what was infinitely more precious to me, than either life or liberty, the pleasure of seeing Madame *de B* * *, and perhaps also the opportunity of even hearing her spoke of. This reflection made me inflexible to the councel of Monsieur *de La***. My people however, continually pressing me to retire to the house of some friend, till I could better dispose of myself. I resolved to communicate my perplexity to *M----* the *Count de* *** my colonel.

WHILE my servant was gone to him with a message from me to that purpose, I received offers of service from
two

two perfons from whom I leaft expected it. My enemy that fame St. *V***,
who came to *Paris* with no other intention than to cut my throat, wrote to
me, that at the follications of his fifter,
he had retired among the fathers of
the convent of ** where under pretence
of a fpiritual retreat, he had been received with much affection: that his
wounds being dangerous, he doubted
not mine were equally fo.---That he
heard the officers of juftice were in
fearch of him, which had furprized
him very much, as he told the furgeon
who had the care of him, that he had
been attacked, either by ftreet-robbers,
or fome unknown enemy: but if the
truth of our combat were known, as
he now fuppofed it was, I had no lefs
to apprehend than himfelf: therefore
wifhed me to fuffer myfelf to be brought
privately to the fame place he had chofe
for his azylum, where we might both
remain in fafety, till the cure of our wounds
were perfected; and afterwards, if we
were fo difpofed, come to an abfolute
decifion of our quarrel.---That far from
having any hatred to me, he was willing

ing to leave the event to fortune.---He added, that I might confide in the bearer of this letter, who would ſerve me as a guide, if I did not chuſe to truſt my own people with my intentions.

I found ſomething very ſingular in the character of *St. V****, but I could not perſuade myſelf, that the precautions he had taken for his ſafety, were equally neceſſary for me: becauſe not only my honour, but my religion, and the law of nature, exacted a defence of my life when attacked. And on this ſcore, the azylum he mentioned, would much better have become me, then it did him ; for I looked upon it as a kind of prophanation to ſhelter a murderous intention, in the boſom of peace and charity. He told me he had taken this retreat at the ſollicitations of his ſiſter ; I found by that ſhe was in *Paris*, and had no reaſon to doubt, but that her ſollicitations alſo, had occaſioned our combat: this, if no other motive would have been ſufficient to have made me avoid a place, where I muſt have been expoſed to the ſight of a perſon, I had ſo little cauſe to be

be pleafed with.   I fent my excufes to
St. V*** for not accepting his offer;
but told him, I did not think I had any
reafon to fear juftice would condemn
the manner in which I had proceeded;
and as to the future defigns he hinted at,
he fhould find me ready to anfwer him
whenever he thought fit to put me again
under the neceffity of defending myfelf.

I had no fooner difpatched his mef-
fenger than I received another letter,
knowing the hand, I was about to fend
it back without reading, but curiofity
prevailing above refentment, I opened
it.   It came from madamoifelle *de St.
V. * * **, and far from the reproaches I
expected, I found it contained only
expreffions of grief and tendernefs. She
protefted to heaven, that though fhe
came to *Paris* with her brother, fhe
was ignorant of his bloody defigns, till
the dreadful moment that fhe faw him
brought to his apartment covered with
wounds, and had learned from himfelf,
that he left me in the fame condition,--
that he had praifed my generofity, and
before he went to the place of his con-
cealment,

cealment, difcovered a great deal of anxiety for my fate. That the officers of juftice had entered his lodging the moment after he had left it; and, that as fhe believed me threatened with the fame danger, begged I would retire from it,---that if I wanted a proper retreat in fuch an affair, it came into her mind, that I might be effectually concealed in her brother's apartment, fince none would think of fearching for me, in a place which belonged to my enemy. --- She added, that if I accepted this offer, I might depend not only upon her honour for protection, but alfo, on every thing in her power, which might contribute to the fpeedy cure of my wounds.

I debated for fome moments, whether I ought to give any anfwer to this letter, or not.---I was even uncertain, by what name I fhould call this medley of hate and affection; the fifter and the brother had equally contrived to perplex me, by their fervices and their outrages.------ The one, had form'd defigns againft my life, the other againft my reputation; I could think no otherwife of the dange-

rous policies of both, than as the cover
of some farther bad intention.---I did
not believe *St. V* * * guilty of perfidy, but I knew he was of violence ;
and though nothing was more distant
from my thoughts, than the real project
of his sister ; yet by what I had experienced of her humour, I thought it behoved me to be upon my guard. The
consideration, however, of her sex, made
me pass over the repugnance I had to
write to her ; but I thought it sufficient
that I thank her in two lines. I then
gave strict orders that my doors should
be shut to all messages or visits, except
my colonel, I may say my best of friends,
whom I impatiently expected.

THIS precaution spared me a very
vexatious scene, Madamoiselle *St. V***
having heard in what circumstances I
was, thought herself authorized by my
situation to make me a visit. Her coach
being stoped at the door, my servants
knowing her livery, ran down to tell
her I was gone for some days into the
country : she could not be persuaded I
could rise and go out in so short a time,

as

as the return of the meſſenger ſhe had
ſent to me : her objections and entreaties were extremely urgent ; but finding
all in vain, retired, as my ſervants told
me, with tears in her eyes. I could not
avoid being ſurprized, but her whole behaviour having always been miſterious. I
did not give myſelf the trouble to dive
into what ſo little touched me. I was
agitated by emotions mere intereſting :
in the uncertainty of my fate, I delibe-
rated whether the friendſhip of Monſieur *de B****, did not oblige me to communicate to him the misfortune that had
fallen on me ; and alſo if I ought not to
let his wife know, that an abſence from
her would be more inſupportable than
all my wounds. The diſcourſe of Monſieur *de La****, had given birth to
hopes, which in myſelf would never
have had ſource. I could find my paſſion augmented by the flattering inter-
pretations of a friend : he had perſuaded
me Madame *de B**** was not without
an inclination for me, and the charming
idea would not depart one moment from
my mind. I recalled to my memory all
that could give it a reſemblance of reality,
till

till by degrees the sweet imagination took
such possession of me, that I already
thought I saw her anxious for my recovery, and trembling for my danger:
but then again, I considered in such a
city as *Paris,* a duel between two officers little known, would scarce be so
much talked of as to reach her ears.---
This thought afterward gave place to a-
nother, I reflected that her husband had
been informed of every particular of my
conduct during my three weeks absence;
and if she remained in ignorance of it
at this time, it must be owing to her
want of attention to the things relating
to me. I was revolving in this manner,
and had not quite determined, whether
it were best for me to attend, till she
should hear of my adventure, from the
mouths of others, or inform her of it
myself; when the footman whom Monsieur *de La* *** had taken with him to
prison, returned with what intelligence
that faithful friend had been able to procure.

He had still continued to pass for
me, and intended to do so, till he should
be

be interrogated by the judge, but renewed his entreaties, that I would not fail taking an immediate refuge in some place of security. He had learned of the officers who had arrested him, that *St. V****, having recovered his speech and senses, at the surgeon's where I had caused him to be carried, had protested, that he was set upon, and wounded by persons unknown. This story being told to the [a] *Archers du Guet*, they employed the remainder of the night in endeavouring to discover the truth. They received intelligence of him at the surgeon's, and some accident making them also find I had a rencounter, orders were given to seize us both. Thus an affair which ought to have appeared wholly in my favour, became more dangerous for me than *St. V****; because they intended to prosecute me as assassin. While I was meditating on the capriciousness of these accidents, the *Count de ****, my colonel, came in, and confirmed all I had been told. On

---

[a] A sort of watchmen, who ride about the streets of *Paris*, to prevent robberies, and all kind of disorders in the night.

the

the firſt news of what had happened
to me, he had run to Monſieur the lieu-
tenant of criminal cauſes, and related
to him the truth of the affair, as he had
heard it from my ſervant, and endeavour
ed to prevail on him to retract the orders
he had given for arreſting me, offering
to be bail for me himelf; but finding
that could not be done, and I was charged with a crime of a blacker nature,
and that the clearing my innocence
would take up a long time, he came
to preſs me to retire. Three days, *added he*, may perhaps be ſufficient to juſtify you, if you are not taken; but
when a perſon is once in the hands of
the law, ways are found to keep him
there longer than is really conſiſtent
with equity. So ſhort a time as he
propoſed, baniſhed from my mind thoſe
reaſons I had againſt leaving *Paris*.
He told me, that if my ſituation would
permit me to take the journey, he
thought I could be no where ſo ſafe as
in our garriſon, on which I reſolved to
go to *Sedan*. I mentioned, however,
Monſieur *de la* ***, but my colonel
told me, I need be under no appre-
hensions,

henfions for that gentleman, who would
be difcharged the moment he appeared
before the judge. My *valet de chambre,*
however, objected, that the motion
in fo long a journey might be dangerous, and that without repofe, and an
exact regimen, he could not anfwer for
my life; but my colonel removed this
difficulty, by offering a litter belonging to a bifhop of *Languedoc,* who was
his near kinfman, and had been brough'.
to *Paris* in it, two days before, for the
recovery of his health. He fent that
inftant to demand it, and his requeft
being granted, it was judged proper I
fhould be carried in my chair to the
farther end of the town, where the litter was to attend. He would have
prevailed upon me to go directly, offering to accompany me a great part of the
way, and was furprized to find me make
pretences for delaying till night, what
feemed to require the greateft expedi-
tion. I have affairs, *faid I,* of the utmoft importance to manage, therefore
entreat you to employ this day in pro-
curing the liberty of Monfieur *de la*
***, and to leave to myfelf the care

of

of making my escape, as you have had
the goodnefs to furnifh me with the
means.

THOSE who know what it is to love,
will eafily comprehend the motive of
this delay : I thought lefs of my wounds,
or of my liberty, or even life, than the
fight of madame *de B* * * * before my
departure. That blefling I thought
would fortify my heart, and enable it
to fuftain the pangs of abfence, and
judging that fhe was yet ignorant of
what had befallen me, I was impatient
to prove what effect it would have on
her, when fhe fhould fee me in the
condition to which I was now reduced.
I fent two of my fervants to the fuburbs, who were to attend me on horfeback, then went into my chair, and my
valet de chambre followed at a diftance,
ordering the men to carry me through
all the lanes and backways they could,
which precaution they obferving, it was
near two hours before I reached the
houfe of Monfieur *de B* * * *. I arrived juft as madame was fitting down to
table. The palenefs of my face, and
the

the neceffity I was under of being fup-
ported by my *valet de chambre,* as I
came up ftairs, and paffed through the
anti-chamber, was fufficient to give her
caufe to imagine fome ill accident had
happened. She took no notice of it in
words, but I could perceive a concern
which came pretty near difquiet in her
countenance. I faluted her gravely, and
having afked leave to fit down, could
not do fo without grimaces, which de-
noted I was in extreme Pain.

MONSIEUR *de B * * **, who had been
fhocked at the change of my looks, and
was now more alarmed at my pofture,
waited not till I had recoverod my
breath to fpeak. Wherefore my dear
count, *faid he*, do you keep your friends
in fufpence. What is the meaning of
this change in you! tell me immediately, I conjure you! I then recounted to him, with a feeble voice, all the
circumftances of my unhappy adventure, concealing only the caufe of quarrel.
I directed my difcourfe wholly to him,
and in fpite of the defign I had to ftudy the emotions of madame *de B * * **,

I

I had not the boldness to turn my eyes
that way, till after I had ended my recital, and received the warmest testimonies of his friendship and affliction.
At last venturing to cast my eyes on the
face of his wife, I found the tenderest
pity painted in it. She seemed indeed
lost in the soft emotion, but she recovered herself immediately, and assumed
an air of more tranquility, though nevertheless she said many obliging things
on my misfortune, and the danger of
the journey I was about to undertake,
alas! *answered I*, I apprehend nothing
but the length of it. As this might be
understood two ways, I know not whether she comprehended my real meaning or not.

OUR conversation was very melancholy, as I was not in a condition to
dine with her, I entreated her to sit
down to table, which she did, but eat
so little, that thinking herself obliged
to make some excuse, she said a violent
head-ach had taken away her appetite.
Her husband inconsolable for my misfortune, and the necessity of my absenting
myself,

myself, proposed all the resources he
could think of; but I found all of them
too dangerous to risque, the offer of his
house, where he imagined I might be
concealed from all the world, was a
temptation from which I could the least
defend myself. I looked on madame
de B ***, and found nothing in her
eyes that shewed a desire of opposing
the proposal he had made; but though
I believed I could no where be more
safe, I considered what was owing to
the honour of Monsieur *de B****, and
was persuaded, that on this occasion,
love and friendship, ought to have the
same scruples; besides the regard my
colonel had shewn for me, made me
think it my duty to depend on his pro-
mises, and follow his advice.

I had only now to have my wounds
new dressed, before I took my leave.
To that end, I asked permission of madame *de B* * **, to retire into the next
room, though her husband would fain
have prevailed upon me, that the ope-
ration might be performed by his bed-
side.

　　　　　　My

My wounds appeared very well, but the fatisfaction of my mind, which perhaps contributed to give them that good colour, made them alfo bleed afrefh, it poured forth in fuch abundance, that I fainted away. My *valet de chambre* crying out for help, madame *de B* * * * being ftill with her hufband, ran haftily out to learn the occafion. She did not fpeak one word, as I was afterwards told, but joining in attempting to recover me with the moft affectionate affiduity, and feemed fo much tranfported at the firft figns I gave of life, that fhe took both my hands, and preffed them between hers.

On my opening my eyes, I was in fuch an extacy at finding her fo near me, and difcovering the pofture fhe was in, that it gave me ftrength to incline my head, and fix my lips on thofe adorable hands: on which fhe made fome efforts to draw back. Ah madam ! *faid I in broken accents, and affembling all my ftrength to retain her,* permit me to enjoy one inftant of happinefs.

pinefs. It was in vain, I had fcarce
ended this exclamation, when fhe was
removed fome paces diftant. And I could
look toward her with the moft pity-
moving eye, as a cruel divinity who rejected my adorations.

SHE was fome moments filent, and I
imagined I faw in her countenance an
uncertainty what anfwer to make; however, after turning to my *valet de cham-*
bre, fhe exhorted him to neglect nothing that might help me. You are
very unjuft, *faid fhe to me, with the*
moft amiable blufh, if you do not regard
me as the moft tender friend you have
in the world. She went out of the
room in fpeaking thefe words, and the
agitation I was in, was very near throwing me into the fame faintings, I was
juft recovered from.

THE fkill of my *valet de chambre*,
and the elixers he gave me, rendered
me able at laft to be led to the bed-fide of
Monfieur *de B* * * *; the account his
wife had given him of my condition,
made him renew his perfuafions not to

quit

quit his houfe; but my *valet de cham-bre*, who had as much concern for my liberty as my health; reprefented to me that there would be no fatigue in a litter, efpecially, as it belonged to an ecclefiaftick, who were always careful to provide for their own eafe. The night being far advanced, he advifed me to take fome hours of repofe, after which he faid, he was certain I fhould find myfelf much better.

I confefs the goodnefs of Madame *de B****, had infpired me with fen-timents, which furprized me more than all the remedies of art.——But I went a-way affoon as I awoke, without feeing her again; fhe had indeed intended to attend my going, in order to judge the better how I fhould go through my journey, and to furnifh me with any thing I might ftand in need of. But in paffing to another apartment, I had exacted a promife both from her, and her hufband, that they would give themfelves no farther trouble on my ac-count at that time.

I N going out of this dear house, could
I have thought, that when I next approached it, I should bring with me
only shame, despair, and horror unut-
terable : such a prodiction would have
appeared vain and impossible to be fulfilled : according to my principles, the
engagement of the heart was equal to
an oath taken before the altar.---I was
not more sure of my existence, than I
was of my inviolable tenderness and
fidelity, and to what fate soever I should
be ordained by heaven, and whatever
revolutions might happen in my fortune, I should be always devoted to
Madame *de B****, and never to any o-
ther.

O N her side, I began to imagine
she was not altogether insensible.---A
tender friendship I knew was all that
was permitted her, and it was all I asked
or wished.---She would not have shewen
so much, if she had not felt yet much
more. Thus all my desires were ac-
complished, the happiness of my life
required no farther, and without div-

G 6 ing

ing into future events, I thought my-self at prefent fo bleft, that from re-garding Monfieur *de B* * * *, with an eye of jealoufy, I rejoiced to leave my treafure under fo fure a guard, whom I could confide in, by the equal fecu-rity of friendfhip and of marriage.

My thoughts were now more calm than of a long time; I even regretted not the fhort abfence I was going to endure, confoled by fuch hopes as I was in a manner authorized to indulge. I got into the litter before day-break, and was a confiderable way on the road when the fun began to fend forth his beams.

I found no other inconvenience than an exceffive heat, occafioned by the weather, and the clofenefs of the ve-hicle I was in.

About evening, I arrived at *Soif-fons*, where I intended to lie that night, but my people informing me that they had taken notice of a man on horfeback, who had followed them at fome dif-tance,

tance, ever since morning, and that having stopped several times, in order that
he might pass them : they were surprized to find him stop also, as if he was
afraid of being known. This intelligence, made me resolve to continue
my journey without taking any other
repose than was necessary to refresh the
horses, and change the dressing my
wounds.

My *valet de chambre* seemed fearful,
left this constant motion should be hurt-
ful to me, but I promised him to lie
still all the next day.

BEING resolved to find out, if possible, the intent of the man, who still
followed, I ordered my two men to
conceal themselves at the entrance of a
wood we were to pass, and rush out
upon him at once.

THIS stratagem succeeded, and they
seized him in spite of the effort he made
to escape by flight, and knowing him for
the same person who had brought the
letter from Madamoiselle *de St. V* * * *,
forced

forced him to come with them to my litter.

I afked him what defign he had in following me, on which he confeffed, that his lady having charged him to difcover the place to which I was going, he had watched in the Street where I lived, and feeing my two fervants go out on horfeback, he had ran after them on foot, to the extremity of the fuburbs, where feeing a litter, and that they alighted, he doubted not, but it was for my coming they waited; on which he hafted to hire a horfe, with a refolution to follow me, if it were to the end of the world. Far from illtreating the fellow, I admired his fidelity and zeal. Your curiofity fhall be fatisfied, *faid I,* if you continue to follow me.

IN fine, I was determined to fuffer him to accompany my people, contenting myfelf with forbidding them to mention where I was going, till he fhould know it by my arrival: thinking it would then be time enough to
confider

confider whither it were beft to fuffer
him to return, or to confine him as
long as I judged proper.

I confented to lie ftill that whole
day, and indeed, my wounds were fo
much inflamed, that my *valet de cham-*
bre told me, he could anfwer for nothing, if I did not yield myfelf abfo-
lutely to his direction. He forced me
to pafs two days and two nights at *Rhe-*
tel ; but found myfelf fo much better
on the third, that I thought I might
purfue my journey without danger : but
on the day of my arrival, was feized
with a violent Fever, which deprived
me of my fenfes. I was without knowledge when they took me out of the
litter, and returned not to myfelf but
to feel the extremeft agonies. My *va-*
let de chambre, frighted at the condition
he faw me in, took off my plaifters
with a trembling hand, and found my
principle wound was fo much enflamed,
that he had little hopes of my life.

THE danger, notwithftanding was fomewhat abated the next day, but though the
fever

fever had given some intermission, it had
not left me. My pains were still the
same, and I had all the reason in the
world to believe, that I had a very little longer time to live, and that I was
at present only supported by the vigour
of my mind, which I found was also
just ready to abandon me.

I often heard those about me whis-
per to each other, that in so raging a
fever as mine, it was a miracle if I a-
voided the gangrene, and I judged by
the frequent observation my *valet de
chambre* made of my wounds, that he
was every moment expecting to discover it.

IT was on the fixth day of this situation, that they told me two priests defired to speak to me in private. I looked on their visit as a pious artifice of
my people, in order, I might fulfil the
last duties of religion, and was far from
being offended at it. Yes, *cried I*, let
them come in, I have reason to wish
their presence. My servants, however,
had no hand in sending for them, but
                              thought

thought as I did, that they came on a very different errand.

THESE ecclefiaftics fat gravely down near my bed, and after fome difcourfe, fuitable to the circumftances I was in, the eldeft of them afked me, if, in the midft of my pains, I had not fome confideration of the rights and griefs of one whofe caufe was put into their care. I doubt not, *faid he*, but you underftand me, otherwife I fhall fpeak more plainly if you confent.

HE was deceived, I underftood fo little of what he meant, that taking thefe expreffions in the fenfe my mind was full of, that is, by fpiritual figures, reprefenting the danger of my condition, and the cares of my foul, I anfwered that I was ready to conform to the duties he propofed. What joyful news, *faid he*, will this be to an unfortunate woman! She fhall immediately come to you, though the fatigues of fo long and hafty a journey have rendered her very weak and faint. I will take on myfelf, *added he*, the care of providing the neceffary

ceſſary diſpenſation, and in the condition you are, my quality of curate
gives me the ſame right as a biſhop.

He was going on the execution of
his deſign, but by this time I had ſufficient comprehended what he meant.---
All the blood that remained in me, now
retired to my heart.---My combat, my
wounds, the imagined near approach of
death, had never wrought in me ſo
ſtrange a revolution.---I collected all my
ſtrength to ſtretch out my arm to pull
him back, and in the difficulty I found
it to ſpeak, retained him more by my
ſigns, than my expreſſions.

When he had ſat down again, I
took a moment of breath, for I had no
need of time to prepare what anſwer I
ſhould give him.---The ſtate I am in,
ſaid I, deſerves more compaſſion.----
Your zeal for the perſon who employs
you, is the moſt barbarous cruelty to a
dying man. I am not inquiſitive into
your motives for undertaking this buſineſs, but will ſuppoſe it proceeds only
from an uprightneſs of heart, and love

of

of juſtice: but know, your endeavouring to inſpire me with falſe terrors, is a vain abuſe of your miniſtry.---That which you propoſe to me in the hour of death, I ſhould have done in the full vigour of my health; if I had looked upon it as a duty.---The hopes of a better life to which I am going, ſerve but to confine me in my former principles.---Retire then, *added I*, if you came hither on no other deſign than what you have mentioned. I ſpoke this with ſo much reſolution, that he did not think proper to preſs me any farther on that ſubject, and only offered me his aſſiſtance in the laſt offices of religion, which I received with all ſubmiſſion to the will of heaven.

THE faintneſs into which I fell after the departure of theſe prieſts, did not hinder me from queſtioning my people concerning the arrival of Mardamoiſelle *St. V****, and reproaching them for taking ſo little care to ſave me from this perſecution: they confeſſed that in the continual terrors they were in for my life, they had loſt ſight of the
courier

courier she had sent after me ; and that afterwards hearing she was at *Sedan*, had not suspected her design. Besides the fears of giving me whatever might disturb my repose, made them several letters they had received for me ; but on the contrary, they would have been glad to have opened them, if they had guessed what they contained.

THE zeal and interest of my friends, had already terminated my affair : the truth of my adventure was declared, and my combat justified by self-defence. My father who came to *Paris*, on a letter my *valet de chambre* had wrote to him without my privity, had joined with my colonel to stop all process against me, and were now upon the road to *Sedan*, in company with Monsieur *de la* ***, who had testified no less impatience, than either of them for my recovery.

I was ignorant how much I owed to parternal tenderness, and the affection of my friends : when towards the evening, I had the inexpressible consolati-

on

on of hearing my fathers voice, and feeling myself preſſed between his arms. He arrived with Monſieur the *Count de**** and Monſieur *de la****, it was not by my eyes that I was capable of knowing them, nor by my words that I could expreſs the ſentiments of my heart. I had not diſtinguiſhed my father, but by the tender complaints that accompanied his embraces. The gangrene now appeared, I began to loſe the uſe of my ſenſes. The ſhades of death came over me, and for above an hour, each breath I drew ſeemed to be the laſt.

ALL the attempts I made to utter ſome few words were intercepted, and nothing but broken and unintelligible ſounds proceeded from me. I had notwithſtanding ſome remains of memory and reaſon: I even perceived that my father was deſired to go into the antichamber. Monſieur *de La****, who in his abſence came cloſe to my bedſide, imagined that if any thing could recall my ſpirits in the mortal weakneſs I was, it would be the name of Madame

de

de *** B, he knew the innocence of my paſſion, and that a virtuous affection ends not but with life, becauſe it is not attended with that remorſe, which in our lateſt moments, if no ſooner, will convince us we have been to blame. I have ſeen Monſieur and Madame *de B***, ſaid he,* with no other deſign than to bring you ſome conſolation; and I am charged with the moſt tender teſti-monies of their friendſhip. He then took my hand, and I preſt his with all the ardor that remained in me, and felt, in hearing him pronounce that dear name, that love would be the laſt emo-tion of my heart.

SOON after this, my father returned, and approached my bed with a ſilence which I imagined was occaſioned only by his grief: but alaſs! it was the black pre-ſage of thoſe misfortunes, that extremi-ty of wretchedneſs, of which he was going to open the ſource: he prayed me to ſummon all my attention, to what he was about to ſay. And then, after having repreſented to me, that my laſt moment was at hand, and that he could

not

not believe me uncertain of my situation, becaufe he knew I had fulfilled all that was required of me, in paffing from this life into another ; *he added*, that he found nothing wanting in my preparations, which the duties of religion injoined ; yet notwithftanding all this, he fhould be glad to fee me exert a superabundance of virtue, in an action worthy of the noblenefs and goodnefs of my character.

I N fine, he reminded me, that the unfortunate Madamofelle St. *V* *** muft be condemned to infamy for her whole life, if pity did not make me confent to leave her my name.—That fhe had entreated it of me, with agonies which had ed even his heart ; and then told me, that it it was of little importance to me, whether I left the world in celibacy or marriage, that is to fay, to carry to the grave, a quality which would alter nothing of my fate ; and he therefore wifhed to prevail on me, to have this complaifance for an unhappy creature, which he faid would render my death precious before god and man, by fixing

the

the well doing of another, at my laſt breath. I doubted not, indeed, but that I was in the arms of death, and each moment of reſpiration ſeemed the laſt effort of nature. My compaſſion, or rather charity, joined with my father's interceſſion, and gained the aſcendent over all my reſolutions.

I preſſed the hand of Monſieur *de La****, to make him comprehend to whom I was devoted in expiring, and then by inclining my head declared to my father, that I would obey his orders. Madamoiſelle St. *V**** and the curate, whom ſhe did not fail to make accompany her, came that inſtant into my chamber, and drew near my bed. I had my eyes cloſed, and thought no more of opening them ; but I permitted the curate to take my hand when he demanded it of me, as the only part of me, that in this caſe I yielded to his miniſtry ; on which, he immediately pronounced the nuptial benediction.

The End of the Second Book.